"I'm damn glad you wer

"Just like you were there
Sloan," Leslie said softly.

Her words made him realize that they'd been there for each other when it had mattered the most. The potential alternative outcome made him shiver.

"You're still cold. I'd better go and get that hot chocolate going," she said, shifting to get up.

"Don't go yet," he said, not ready for any distance to be put between them or their bodies.

She glanced over at him. Their gazes held before she said, "You do know the only reason why we're in this sleeping bag together, right?"

He nodded. "Yes. Because I needed your body's heat last night." He inched his mouth closer to hers and then said, "Only problem is, I still need your body's heat, Les. But now I need it for a totally different reason."

And then he leaned in and kissed her...

* * *

What He Wants for Christmas
by Brenda Jackson is part of the
Westmoreland Legacy: The Outlaws series.

BRENDA JACKSON

WHAT HE WANTS FOR CHRISTMAS

HARLEQUIN

DESIRE

HARLEQUIN®

DESIRE™

Recycling programs
for this product may
not exist in your area.

ISBN-13: 978-1-335-73528-7

What He Wants for Christmas

Copyright © 2021 by Brenda Streater Jackson

This edition published by arrangement with Harlequin Books S.A.

For questions and comments about the quality of this book,
please contact us at CustomerService@Harlequin.com.

Harlequin Enterprises ULC
22 Adelaide St. West, 40th Floor
Toronto, Ontario M5H 4E3, Canada
www.Harlequin.com

Printed in U.S.A.

Brenda Jackson is a *New York Times* bestselling author of more than one hundred romance titles. Brenda lives in Jacksonville, Florida, and divides her time between family, writing and traveling. Email Brenda at authorbrendajackson@gmail.com or visit her on her website at brendajackson.net.

Visit her Author Profile page at Harlequin.com, or brendajackson.net, for more titles.

You can also find Brenda Jackson on Facebook, along with other Harlequin Desire authors, at Facebook.com/harlequindesireauthors!

To the man who will always and forever be the love of my life and the wind beneath my wings, Gerald Jackson, Sr.

Wishing everyone the best of the holidays.

To all my readers who love the Westmorelands and Outlaws. This book is for you.

With thanks to Diaminique Watson and Mahogany Mitchell for sharing information on North Pole, Alaska, and Fairbanks, Alaska. Your time and the information were greatly appreciated.

Judge not, and ye shall not be judged: condemn not, and ye shall not be condemned: forgive, and ye shall be forgiven.

—*Luke* 6:37

One

Sloan Outlaw whipped his head around. He would recognize that voice anywhere. There were some things he'd never forget, like the sound of the woman who had broken his heart ten years ago.

He couldn't stop his eyes from scanning the crowd of people, who, like him, were attending the wedding celebration for Tyler and Keosha. Within moments, he had spotted her.

Leslie Cassidy.

There she stood, regal, sophisticated and as beautiful as ever with her bedroom brown eyes, mocha-colored skin, a pair of full lips, high cheekbones and short hair. He blinked. Short hair? What happened to that glorious mass of dark brown curls that used to flow around her shoulders? The same hair he'd loved running his fingers through whenever they made love? Whenever she'd cuddled in his arms, whenever they did just about anything? The curls were gone. However, he would admit the short style looked cute on her. Sassy and chic. It showed a degree of maturity and modishness that defined her strikingly gorgeous features. He couldn't help but think the short style made her look even sexier.

His gaze raked down the rest of her. She still possessed a body that made men take a second look. Those legs were the most gorgeous pair he'd ever seen on a woman. He could clearly remember how she would wrap them around him tight whenever they made love. The sexiness of her above-the-knee dress not only show-cased those legs but also emphasized every single curve she possessed.

Leslie had always been an attention grabber, and from the number of guys he saw checking her out, it seemed nothing had changed. He should have known she would be here. After all, like him, she was friends of both the bride and groom from their college days at the University of Alaska at Anchorage. And yet he honestly hadn't thought about running into her. He had deliberately blocked her from his mind over the years. He would always have an issue with her believing a lie about him, when she of all people should have trusted him beyond any doubt.

Instead, she hadn't given him a chance to defend himself. She'd left the university, only sending him an email, the contents of which still burned when he thought about them. The first line had read, *I hate you.* It hadn't taken long for him to find out why—she had believed the lies of her roommate. The same woman she'd thought was her best friend. The same woman who'd tried coming on to him behind Leslie's back. If anything, his mistake had been in thinking he could handle the situation and not involve Leslie by telling her of Sarah Olsen's behavior. Had he told her, then Leslie would have been prepared for the woman's lies. But he hadn't, and in the end, Leslie had believed the worst.

More people had arrived at the wedding celebration. The ballroom of the hotel in Juneau was crowded, and now his view of Leslie was obstructed. Just as well. Still, Tyler should have warned him she was coming. He intended to give his frat brother and good friend a piece of his mind for not doing so.

As Sloan stood there nursing a glass of champagne, he knew he was ill-equipped to deal with seeing the one and only woman he had ever loved.

"Well, have you seen him yet?"

Leslie Cassidy turned and looked into the face of her best friend, Carmen Golan. When Leslie had left the University of Alaska at Anchorage, she had transferred to Howard University in DC to be close to her aunt Ella, her father's only sister. At least that's the reason she'd told everyone. Carmen had been her roommate at Howard and was one of the most positive people she knew. Her friend's optimism had helped Leslie get through some rough times after her breakup with Sloan.

"No, I have not seen him, and I'm not looking for him, Carmen."

"Well, you should. You owe him an apology."

There were days Leslie wished Carmen had not been with her that night three years ago when they'd taken a girls' trip to LA. At a nightclub they had run into Sarah Olsen, of all people, the woman who'd been Leslie's roommate while at college in Alaska. It was obvious Sarah had had one too many drinks, and in a drunken spiel she had bragged about how her plan to deliberately break up Leslie and Sloan had worked.

She'd even made fun of Leslie in front of everyone for being gullible enough to believe Sarah's lies. That was when Leslie realized all those things she had believed about Sloan had not been true.

"I will eventually see him, Carmen, but I don't intend to go looking for him. There're over a couple hundred guests here."

What she wouldn't mention to Carmen was that the phone call she'd gotten from her attorney before leaving the hotel was weighing more heavily on her mind than an apology to Sloan right now.

"I would help find him if I knew what he looked like."

She was glad Carmen didn't know, because there was no doubt in Leslie's mind that Carmen would go looking for Sloan. "He might not have come."

The disappointment in Carmen's eyes made Leslie feel bad for even suggesting such a thing. Her friend believed in taking any opportunity to right a wrong. Carmen was also a hopeless romantic. That's one of the reasons Leslie had asked Carmen to attend the wedding with her as her plus-one. Weddings were right up Carmen's alley. Carmen had flown to Alaska to spend

Thanksgiving with Leslie, and her best friend had then also agreed to attend the wedding because it would be the perfect opportunity for Leslie to apologize to Sloan.

Leslie knew Carmen was also hoping she and Sloan could reconcile a relationship that should not have ended in the first place. Leslie had told Carmen countless times that ten years had passed. These days, saving her company from the clutches of Martin Longshire weighed more heavily on her mind than reuniting with Sloan.

"Didn't the bride tell you that she'd gotten Sloan's RSVP saying he would be attending?"

Yes, Keosha had said that. "Yes, however, something could have come up."

A part of Leslie knew that no matter what she'd just said to Carmen, somewhere in this crowd of attendees was Sloan Outlaw. He was here. She could feel his presence.

Sloan knew it would be close to impossible to grab even a minute of Tyler's time since he was the groom and taking wedding pictures. That sent Sloan in search of Redford St. James.

Sloan could forgive Tyler for not mentioning Leslie's attendance to him, since he'd probably had a lot on his mind in preparing for the wedding, but there was no excuse for Redford. If Tyler knew, then so had Redford. During their college days, the three of them had been thick as thieves, and although they now lived in different cities in Alaska, they still found time to get together twice a year.

Moving in and around several people—some he knew, others he did not—Sloan figured that even in this crowd he would have no problem finding Redford. All he needed to do was figure out the best place an amorous couple could engage in a quickie. That sort of thing was what Redford had always been good at, even when they were in college. Storage closets, empty classrooms, underneath the stairs—those were just a few places that easily came to mind.

Sloan left the ballroom and headed down a side corridor toward the back. When a woman rounded the corner and quickly walked past him while trying to straighten her outfit and hair, Sloan knew Redford St. James had struck again. His friend had a problem with keeping his pants zipped.

When Sloan reached a cracked door, he slowly opened it and entered a small meeting room. Redford had his back to him, putting on his jacket.

"I thought I'd find you in here, Redford."

Redford jerked around and then glared at him. "Damn, Sloan, you almost gave me heart failure. I thought you were that woman's boyfriend."

Sloan lifted an eyebrow and then crossed his arms over his chest. "Boyfriend? When did you start trespassing on another man's territory?"

Redford gave him a smooth grin. "When she looked my way a few times and deliberately licked her lips. I figured someone wasn't taking care of her properly, and I got the message. The opportunity was too good to pass up."

"Whatever," Sloan said, closing the door behind him.

"So why didn't you tell me Leslie would be coming to the wedding?"

Redford rolled his eyes. "Did you honestly think she wouldn't be invited? Leslie and Keosha were good friends in college."

"I didn't know they'd stayed in touch over the years."

"No reason they wouldn't, Sloan. You're the only one who considered Leslie an enemy. In fact, if you recall, you forbade me and Tyler to even mention her name around you, so we didn't. Hell, man, we told you what you should have done after that time Sarah came on to you. She was just trouble waiting to happen."

"Okay, maybe I should have said something about it to Leslie, but regardless, Leslie should have trusted me and not believed Sarah."

"Well, that was a pretty convincing lie, and Sarah had proof to back it up, Sloan."

"Regardless, Leslie should have known I was not texting or calling Sarah behind her back, no matter what Sarah's phone records showed."

"I still say you should have warned her about Sarah, so you share the blame as well."

Sloan didn't like it that Redford's thought mirrored his brothers'. They had liked Leslie and felt he should have told Leslie about Sarah, even though Sarah had promised it wouldn't happen again.

"I guess you heard about her father," Redford said, breaking into his thoughts.

Sloan lifted a brow. "No, what about her old man?"

"He died three months ago."

Sloan hadn't known. "I'm sorry to hear that. Was he ill?"

"It was a sudden heart attack."

He could just imagine how hard that must have been on Leslie. She and her father had been close. Her mother had died years ago when Leslie had been in her teens. "Who's running the company?" Leslie's father had been founder and CEO of Cassidy Cosmetics, an Alaska-based company whose products were sold directly to stores in the state.

"Leslie's in charge of things now, but I don't know how long that will last."

Sloan frowned. "What do you mean?"

"I'd rather not say, because you have no reason to care. Look, Sloan, we need to go back or Tyler will wonder where we are."

"So now you're worried about being absent from the wedding celebration? Tyler won't care where we are since he's all wrapped up in Keosha, so what's happening with Leslie that I have no reason to care about, Redford? What aren't you telling me?"

Redford sighed, giving in. "Martin Longshire plans to take over her company. He and Leslie's father were longtime enemies, and since her father is dead, he plans to make Leslie pay. Two weeks ago, I slept with a woman who works for Longshire, and she told me. Apparently, the people who work for him can't keep a secret—or the man doesn't give a damn who knows what he plans to do to Leslie."

"Did you tell her?" Sloan asked.

"No, not yet. But I did tell Tyler and Keosha. Keosha

said she would warn Leslie about it, but I doubt it will do any good. Everybody knows Martin Longshire is a bastard. If he did have a beef with Leslie's father, then he has no problem making her suffer because of it."

Sloan didn't say anything as he and Redford returned to the ballroom. He silently told himself anything dealing with Leslie was not his business.

"I'll be back, man," Redford said. "Telling you what Longshire plans to do to Leslie has left a bad taste in my mouth. I need a stiff drink." He then quickly walked toward the bar.

As Sloan watched his friend leave, the hairs on the back of his neck stood up. He immediately knew who was standing behind him even before she spoke.

"Hello, Sloan."

He turned to stare right into Leslie's face.

Two

"How are you, Leslie?"

Leslie knew the man towering in front of her was every bit of six two, and her five-foot, eight-inch height didn't reach his chin even in her stilettos. But his height wasn't what had her heart pounding and pulse racing.

Ten years ago, Sloan Outlaw was considered extremely handsome. By today's standards he was that ten times over. And he wore a suit better than any man she knew. He'd always been a sharp dresser, even in college, when he'd had the preppy style down to an art form. Even now his jacket embraced a pair of masculine shoulders while covering the broadness of his chest. Her gaze lowered to the zipper of his pants, and she recalled all the times she would ease it down. He loved whenever she undressed him, and she had loved it as well. She had never regretted sharing his bed…except for when she thought he'd betrayed her with Sarah.

After Sarah's drunken boast, Leslie had thought about contacting Sloan to apologize. Locating him would not have been difficult, since his family's freight line was a successful one in Alaska. However, considering how she'd broken things off between them, leaving town without letting him know where she'd gone and then sending him a nasty email, Leslie had figured she was the last person he would want to hear from, even if it was to apologize.

She had looked him up on social media. In addition to being the handsome man he'd always been, Sloan Outlaw was now successful in his own right. Not only did he work in the day-to-day operations of his family's multimillion-dollar business, he was involved with several of his own companies, including a foundation he'd established a few years ago. He gave of his time and money, which meant Sloan was still the generous and caring guy she had known and fallen in love with at nineteen.

Leslie noted that he also gave of his time to the opposite sex. He'd been captured in a number of photos with beautiful women on his arm while attending several high-profile events. But he hadn't married yet. She found it hard to believe that someone hadn't snatched him up by now. Just looking into the darkness of his chocolate-colored eyes and seeing those well-defined lips was making it hard to breathe. He'd had that impact on her from the first.

"I'm fine, Sloan. You look well," she finally found her voice to say.

She didn't miss the way his gaze drifted over her. The same way hers had done to him. "And so do you."

Electricity sizzled through her veins just from hearing the sound of his voice. Now was not the time or the place, but was she really surprised when Sloan had always had this sort of effect on her?

"I'm happy for Tyler and Keosha," she said, not able to break eye contact with him, although she knew she should.

"Hell, it took them long enough."

Leslie fought back a smile, because he was right. Tyler and Keosha had been high school sweethearts who'd refused to go to different universities like their parents had suggested. Instead, they had ended up together at University of Alaska at Anchorage.

They'd dated all through college and had been the perfect couple. After college they had returned to Juneau and worked for their families' corporations, satisfied to live together. They saw no rush in getting married, to the dismay of their parents. Tyler and Keosha always said they loved each other and didn't need a piece of paper to prove it. Now they were ready to start a family and felt they should do so as husband and wife.

The couple had refused to give in to the pressures of both sets of parents, who wanted a huge, over-the-top wedding. The bride and groom had preferred a small wedding. When the planning of the large wedding was getting on both their nerves, Tyler and Keosha had taken matters into their own hands and eloped to Vegas just days ago.

Those who'd showed up today discovered they would be attending a wedding celebration instead of a ceremony.

"Well, I guess you can say they got married when they felt the time was right. Just look at them now."

Their gazes traveled across the room to the couple, who were smiling brightly while taking pictures. "They are happy," Sloan said, returning his gaze to her.

The moment their eyes reconnected, she recalled how it felt being touched by Sloan's strong hands. Being stroked by them. Caressed in places that could take her breath away.

She felt a tightness in her throat. "Yes, they are," she agreed. She needed to say what she needed to say before Carmen returned from the dance floor. "I need to talk to you, Sloan."

She saw his face tighten when he said, "You're talking to me now."

She swallowed deeply. They were standing off to the side, where it wasn't crowded. That afforded them some privacy, at least. "I ran into Sarah three years ago, and she told me the truth."

"And what truth was that, Leslie?"

She drew in a deep breath, knowing he would not make this easy for her—and frankly, she couldn't blame him. "The truth that you had not slept with her behind my back."

"I would have told you that if you'd given me the chance."

Yes, he would have, but she had left town without letting him know where she was going, and she had forbidden her father from telling him as well. When she had reached her aunt's house in DC, the first thing she'd done was send Sloan that email, and it hadn't been nice. And then in anger, she had deleted his replies without even reading them as well as blocking his calls.

"I owe you an apology, Sloan."

"Yes, you do." The gaze holding hers was hard, unwavering, and she saw the snarl that curled his lip.

"I apologize."

He didn't say anything for a moment, then he said, "Apology accepted."

His features were hard and unyielding. The one thing she knew about Sloan was that he didn't forgive easily. For him, forgiving did not mean forgetting, excusing or reconnecting. He was a man who loved deeply and cherished friendships until trust was destroyed. By not believing in him, she had destroyed his trust in her beyond repair.

"Thank you for accepting my apology." She felt compelled to say it, although she knew his words had merely been lip service.

"I heard about your father. I offer my condolences. I liked him," he said, propelling the conversation to another topic.

There was no need to tell him that Lester Cassidy had liked Sloan, too. In fact, when she told her father what happened, he had strongly suggested she hear Sloan's side of the story. She hadn't, and now she wished she had taken her father's advice.

"How is your family?" she asked to change the subject. She had met his father, four brothers and sister when he had invited her to his home for Christmas one year. They had all been nice people, although his father had acted sort of reserved.

"Everyone is fine. Garth and Cash are married, Maverick is still happily single, and Charm is still Charm. Jess is a United States senator."

"I know, I voted for him."

He lifted a brow. "You've been back in Alaska for a while?"

"Yes. I moved back to Wasilla two years ago to help Dad run the company."

He nodded and glanced at his watch before looking back at her. "It was good seeing you again, Leslie. I need to let Redford, Tyler and Keosha know I'm leaving. I'm flying to the lower forty-eight in the morning for Thanksgiving."

She noted he didn't tell her which state. It wasn't any of her business. "It was good seeing you again, too, Sloan."

She watched him walk over to where Redford St. James was talking to a group of guys. She was glad she'd gotten the chance to apologize to Sloan. Although that meant closure, it also meant accepting that some things were never meant to be.

"What's wrong with you, Sloan?"

Sloan glanced up at his brother Garth, the oldest of his siblings. He and his family had returned to the office today after spending Thanksgiving at his brother

Cash's ranch in Wyoming. This year they were joined by their cousins, the Westmorelands.

"What makes you think something is wrong with me?"

Garth leaned back in his chair and smiled. "The meeting ended a few minutes ago. Everyone has left the conference room, but you're still sitting here."

Sloan glanced around the room. Yes, he was. He then glanced back at Garth, gave him a cocky grin and said, "So are you."

"Only because I figured you might want to talk."

Sloan lifted a brow. "About what?"

"Anything. I noticed you weren't your usual chipper self over Thanksgiving, either. Is everything going okay with your new position within the company?"

Cash's marriage to Brianna had caused a shifting of job duties at the family's multimillion-dollar company, Outlaw Freight Lines, which was located here in Fairbanks. To accommodate Cash's permanent move to Black Crow, Wyoming, they had established a satellite office of Outlaw Freight Lines on Cash's ranch. Cash now handled the company's expansion into various other states in the lower forty-eight.

Sloan, who had been in charge of international sales and marketing, had replaced Cash in the office to assist Garth in the day-to-day running of the operation. His youngest brother, Maverick, had been more than happy to take over Sloan's former position in charge of international sales. Their brother Jess had been the company's executive attorney until he'd decided to run for political office two years ago. Now as Senator Jessup

Outlaw, he lived most of the time in the nation's capital. Twenty-five-year-old Charm was their only sister. As far as what Charm's duties were at the company, the jury was still out on that one. At the moment they'd given her a job mainly to keep her out of their hair.

"No. I like my duties just fine."

"Glad to hear it. You know if there's ever an issue with anything, you can talk to me about it. That includes any problems with Bart."

Sloan chuckled. He and his siblings knew their father, Bart Outlaw, could be a handful and usually was. The reason Garth was now running the company was because Bart had been forced into retirement. It was either that or be ousted by the board.

It was no secret that Bart had been married five times and that each of his sons had different mothers. It also wasn't a secret that some of those wives had been full-fledged gold diggers. Somehow Bart had managed, and quite manipulatively and underhandedly, they figured, to obtain custody of all five of his sons from his ex-wives. Things had been a little different with Charm's mother, Claudia. To this day, Claudia was the only woman Bart had ever truly loved. And she'd been the only one Bart had not married…but not for lack of trying on his part. Hell, he was still trying.

Bart hadn't known Claudia was pregnant with Charm when their six-month romantic fling had ended and she had taken off for parts unknown. Fifteen years later, Claudia reappeared with Charm in tow, telling Bart that Charm was his child and Claudia couldn't handle the sassiness of the daughter he hadn't known about.

She'd given custody to Bart and told him he could deal with Charm now. Bart's idea of dealing with Charm was spoiling her rotten. It had taken the brothers, especially Garth, to let Charm know they wouldn't tolerate her unruly attitude. Charm quickly fell in line and now adored the five older brothers she hadn't known she had.

"Sloan?"

He glanced over at Garth. "What?"

"You're daydreaming again."

Had he been? Probably so. Sloan paused but then decided to discuss with Garth what had been on his mind since he had spoken to Redford at the wedding. As much as he wanted to dismiss it from his mind, he couldn't, so he definitely could use someone else's perspective.

"I saw Leslie Cassidy at Tyler and Keosha's wedding celebration."

Garth nodded, then asked, "How did that go?"

He knew why Garth was asking. Everyone knew how much he'd cared for Leslie and how badly he had taken their breakup. "It was fine. She finally found out the truth and apologized."

"Better late than never, I guess."

"Yes, better late than never."

Garth studied him. "I take it there's something else."

Sloan nodded. "Have you ever heard of a businessman by the name of Martin Longshire?"

Garth shook his head. "I can't say that I have. Who is he?"

"A bastard."

Garth chuckled. "Will you tell me how you really feel, Sloan?"

Sloan chuckled as well. "I just did."

"Then maybe you ought to tell me why you feel that way."

Sloan told Garth about the conversation with Redford. He could tell by his older brother's facial expressions that he didn't like what he was hearing.

"Did you get a chance to talk to Leslie about it when you saw her at the wedding reception?" Garth asked.

"No. I figured it wasn't my business."

"Like hell" was Garth's quick reply. "If what Redford told you is true, then that's alarming. No man should deliberately target a woman just because of a beef he had with her father. You're right. Longshire is a bastard."

A smiled spread across Sloan's lips. "So tell me how you really feel, Garth."

Garth didn't say anything for a minute and then he asked, "Cassidy Cosmetics is still headquartered in Wasilla, right?"

"Yes, what of it?"

"Nothing. I was just asking." Garth paused. "You still plan to take December off?"

Since Sloan hadn't taken any time off this year, Garth had suggested he take off the entire month of December. Normally this time around the holidays would be the freight lines' busiest, but thanks to Cash's satellite office, road transportation was doing great, since the weather in the lower forty-eight had been pretty good this year. All the domestic freight trucks were delivering ahead of schedule for the Christmas season.

"Yes, that's the plan. I'm looking forward to spending a week or two at the cabin on Kodiak Island before joining everyone in Westmoreland country for Christmas."

It still amazed Sloan how their Westmoreland cousins, whom they'd met only a few years ago, could be such an intricate part of their lives now. The Westmorelands and the Outlaws enjoyed getting together as if to make up for that period of time they hadn't known about each other. "Those plans can be changed if you think I'm needed here, Garth."

Garth shook his head. "No, you won't be needed here. However, considering what Redford told you about Leslie's company, I'd think you might be needed elsewhere."

Sloan held his brother's gaze, knowing what Garth was alluding to. "Why should I even care what happens to Leslie or her company?"

Instead of answering him, Garth stood and walked out of the conference room. Sloan didn't have to wonder why his brother hadn't answered. In Garth's mind, Sloan's question didn't dignify a response.

Three

Leslie glanced up from the papers on her desk when she heard the buzzer. "Yes, Beverly?"

"Mr. Longshire is here to see you, Ms. Cassidy."

Leslie scowled. That man was the last person she wanted to see. Just that morning, Stan Middlebury, her company's attorney, had given her an update, so she knew everything Martin Longshire was up to. The man was intent on taking her company away from her.

She was still catching up on paperwork that had piled up when she'd been out of the office attending Tyler and Keosha's wedding celebration. Carmen had left yesterday to return to DC, and Leslie was missing her already.

"I don't recall Mr. Longshire having an appointment, so I'm unable to meet with him today, Beverly."

"I will let him know."

Before Leslie could go back to reviewing the documents she'd been reading, she heard Beverly's loud voice say, "Wait just a minute. You can't just barge into Ms. Cassidy's office." Her door flew open, and Martin Longshire stood there, looking like the monster Leslie thought him to be.

"Do you want me to contact security, Ms. Cassidy?" asked a flustered Beverly Neal, who'd also been Leslie's father's personal assistant for years.

Leslie stood and came around her desk. "No, Beverly, that won't be necessary. I can handle Mr. Longshire."

Beverly gave her a look that said she wasn't sure, but she nodded anyway. She was about to turn to leave when Mr. Longshire barked at Beverly, "Start cleaning out your desk. When I take over this company, you will be one of the first people I fire."

Instead of responding to what the man said, Beverly walked out, but she did not close the door behind her. Martin Longshire angrily slammed it shut. He then turned his attention back to Leslie. "So, you think you can handle me?"

"Don't you ever talk rudely to my employees again, Mr. Longshire."

The man had the nerve to smirk. "I do whatever the hell I please, and they won't be your employees for long. Like I just told the woman, I'm taking over this company, and there's nothing you can do about it. I'm sure you've heard of my plans by now."

Leslie drew in a deep breath. She had to believe there was something she could do. She didn't have the capital to fight him. As a last-ditch effort, her company attorney was working with several banks to see if one would be willing to give her a loan or extend the ones she had.

"You will never own my company," she said with a lot more confidence than she actually felt.

"We shall see. In the meantime, enjoy the holidays, because they will be the last you'll have here at Cassidy Cosmetics." He turned and walked out of her office.

On weak knees, Leslie made it back around her desk to sit down. She held her head in her hands, but she refused to cry. Her father had taught her to be stronger than that. The last time a man had made her cry had been when she had believed Sloan had betrayed her. At the time, unknowingly, she'd been crying for nothing because he'd been innocent.

"Are you okay, Leslie?"

She glanced up and saw Beverly standing in the doorway with deep concern in her features. She sat up in her chair. The last thing she wanted was for her employees to think she didn't have things under control, although, honestly, she didn't. Because of his intense dislike of her father, Martin Longshire wanted to destroy her.

"Yes, Beverly, I'm fine. And I regret that Mr. Longshire talked to you that way."

"He doesn't scare me any," Beverly said. "As your father's personal assistant, I've had my run-ins with Martin Longshire before." She paused. "Is there anything that I can do?"

Leslie shook her head and forced a smile. "No. What I need is a Christmas miracle."

Beverly nodded. "Well, tomorrow is officially the first of December, so we're going to hope we get that miracle. We have a month." Beverly left, closing the door behind her.

Leslie leaned back in her chair. In reality, they had less time than that. Keeping with the tradition established by her father years ago, Cassidy Cosmetics closed for the holidays on the seventh of December every year and didn't reopen until the second week of January. December ninth had been her mother's birthday, and January fourth had been her father's. All the employees enjoyed the time off with pay. Now according to Mr. Longshire, neither she nor her employees would have a company to return to, since he'd made it known he planned to fire everyone.

Her employees knew the dire straits of the company, but for some reason they believed she would fight and win. After all, she was her father's daughter, and he'd been in sticky situations before and managed to get the company out of it. However, this was more than just a mere sticky situation. This was a hostile takeover by Longshire Industries.

Needing to switch her mind off Martin Longshire, she thought of Sloan Outlaw. At least she had apologized for believing Sarah's lies, and she felt good about that. A weight had been lifted off her chest.

So why had she been thinking about him a lot since the wedding? Well, one reason could be that seeing him again had made her realize what not trusting him had cost her. Being in his presence had pushed a lot of her passion points, ones she'd thought dead and gone. His look alone had made heat settle all through her. Now she felt her stomach flutter at the memory.

But she couldn't indulge in fantasies. Knowing she had plenty of work to do, Leslie turned her attention back to the documents on her desk.

Sloan entered the building that housed Cassidy Cosmetics. The first time he'd come here had been to meet Leslie's father. It had been her first year at the university, and her father had asked her to come home to accompany him to a benefit being held in her mother's honor.

She'd told him on the plane flight from Anchorage to Wasilla that her mother, who had passed away of cancer when Leslie was fourteen, had been active in a number of community and charitable events, and the city of Wasilla would be giving her the recognition she deserved.

By the end of the weekend, he'd mentally compared Leslie's father with his own and seen how vastly different the two men were. Where Bart had a brash countenance, it was easy to see Lester Cassidy had been a people person, and he had made Sloan feel right at home. He'd even made Sloan comfortable while being interrogated. The older man had wanted to get to know Sloan since he would be a part of his daughter's life.

As Sloan stepped into the elevator, his thoughts shifted to his first job at Outlaw Freight Lines—a company researcher. He'd put his skill to work to investigate not only Longshire but also Cassidy Cosmetics. He'd wanted to come up with the best plan to protect Leslie's company against Martin Longshire's hostile takeover.

The proposal he would offer Leslie was a fair one. But would she accept it with the condition he'd attached? Bottom line, he wasn't giving her a choice in the matter if she wanted to save her company. Besides, she owed him. She might have forgotten about it, but he hadn't. And if she had forgotten, now was a good time to refresh her memory.

He got off the elevator on the fifth floor, and it seemed he had walked straight into a Christmas wonderland. The lit tree was beautifully decorated, and there were candy canes hanging from the ceiling. A huge replica of Santa was surrounded by nearly life-size reindeer. All eight of them. Santa was carrying a huge silver case that advertised Cassidy Cosmetics. The display was right on point for the holidays and the company's seasonal promotions.

From the research he'd done, it appeared Leslie had done a good job of handling things since taking over. Her employees loved and respected her. It seemed her only problem was Martin Longshire, who was making an ass of himself. Sloan doubted Leslie was aware of all the underhanded things the man was doing. Well, Sloan was prepared to throw a monkey wrench in those plans if Leslie agreed with his proposal. The decision would be hers.

"May I help you?"

He smiled at the older woman sitting at the desk. "Yes. I'm here to see Leslie Cassidy."

"And who are you, sir?"

"Sloan Outlaw."

The woman studied him curiously, and Sloan had a feeling that just like Helen, their personal assistant at Outlaw Freight Lines who'd worked for them for years, this woman had also taken on the role of guard dog. "Please have a seat, Mr. Outlaw. I'll see if Ms. Cassidy is free to see you."

Sloan nodded and took a seat in one of the chairs across the room. His gaze stayed glued to the woman as she picked up the phone and began speaking. Before she could disconnect the line, the door with Leslie's name flew open. A look of total surprise was on her face. "Sloan?"

He stood. "Yes?"

His gaze traveled over her. If he thought she'd looked good when he'd seen her at the wedding celebration, she looked doubly so now. She was wearing a midi-length green dress with a belt that hugged her small waist. The hem of her dress swished around a pair of black suede boots when she walked. His gaze went back to her short hair again. The more he saw the style on her, the more he liked it.

"What are you doing here?"

Sloan was about to answer, but he glanced over at the woman sitting behind the desk, who wasn't even pretending not to listen to their conversation. He then looked back at Leslie. "I need to speak with you privately."

She held his gaze for a long moment before nodding. "Please come into my office."

He followed her, noticing the sway of her shapely

backside. Some things couldn't be helped, and he'd always had a thing for Leslie's ass. But then, he'd adored the entire package, including that mind of hers. Pushing the memory away, he knew he had to stay focused. The only reason he was here was because he knew it was the right thing to do. Whether she saw it that way would be up to her.

Closing the door behind them, he glanced around, not surprised to see that she had her very own decorated tree in her office. And it wasn't a small one. But then, he shouldn't be surprised. Christmas had always been Leslie's favorite holiday.

"So, what's this about, Sloan?"

He glanced over at her and saw the questioning look on her face. She had to be wondering why he was there. After all, they had gone ten years without seeing each other, and then they had run into each other at a wedding celebration and now he was here, in her city, her territory, her space. She had to know how far he'd traveled to get here. It wasn't like Fairbanks and Wasilla were in close proximity.

"May I sit down?" he asked her.

"Yes, of course."

He watched her move around her desk to sit in the chair behind it. Then he eased down in the chair across from her.

She placed her entwined hands in the middle of her desk and looked at him expectantly.

"It was good seeing you at Tyler and Keosha's wedding celebration."

"It was good seeing you, too, Sloan, but I'm sure you didn't travel to Wasilla just to tell me that."

No, he hadn't. "I'd think my being here would be pretty obvious, Leslie."

She tilted her head the way she always did when confused about something. "Sorry, Sloan, but I have no idea why you're here."

He leaned back in his chair. "I know about your problems with Martin Longshire."

He saw surprise light her eyes. "And what does that have to do with you?"

Good question. Every once in a while he asked himself that same thing. He would tell her the answer he always came up with. "I always liked your father, and I refuse to sit by and let Martin Longshire destroy the company he worked so hard to build."

"So, you're here because of my father?"

He didn't say anything for a minute. Then he decided to be totally honest with her. "Not entirely. You and I were friends once, Leslie. In fact, there was a time when we were more than friends, and I want to help."

She released what sounded like a frustrated breath. "I doubt there's anything you can do at this point, Sloan. I talked to my company attorney a few hours ago, and the picture he painted for me is pretty grim. It seems Mr. Longshire has been working on his revenge since even before Dad died. He's scared off my lenders, and my distributors are beginning to freak out as well. Sales are down because several stores that normally carry our products are not doing so."

All of what she said had been revealed in Sloan's research. What he hadn't found out was why. What was motivating Martin Longshire to destroy Cassidy Cosmetics? "What sort of beef did Longshire have with your father that makes him so determined to take over Cassidy Cosmetics, Leslie?"

She gazed into his eyes for several long moments before saying, "My mother."

Sloan lifted a brow. "Your mother?"

"Yes. Martin Longshire was the man my maternal grandparents selected for their daughter to marry, but my father, a man considered not part of an upstanding social class, was the man she loved. One night, a few months before the wedding was to take place, she eloped and married my father instead. As a result, there was a scandal. For years my grandparents disowned my mother, and Martin Longshire despised them both. I'm not sure he ever loved my mother, but he saw her as a possession he wanted. Was entitled to have. According to my father, the scandal lasted for a while, and it was embarrassing to Mr. Longshire. He moved out of the country to head up his family business in Paris for a few years. He returned fifteen years ago and has been causing my father grief ever since."

Sloan recalled her telling him years ago that her maternal grandparents had died when she was a little girl of ten. He further recalled her saying she'd had a close relationship to them. "Because you and your grandparents were close, I assume they finally accepted your parents' marriage."

"Yes. They saw how happy Dad made my mother—

and how mean Martin Longshire turned out to be—
and were glad Mom hadn't married him." She paused
then added, "That's why Longshire wants to destroy the
company my parents started together. He sees doing so
as the ultimate revenge."

Sloan shook his head. "The man sounds demented."

"Yes, that may be the case. He's been planning it
for a long time, and with Dad's death, he sees the opportunity."

Drawing in a deep breath, she pushed back from the
desk. "In fact, I'm getting my employees together later
today to prepare them for the worst. When this office
closes for the holidays on Friday, there's a possibility it
might reopen in January under new management. Right
now, I'm doing all I can to make sure their pensions
are protected, since Longshire plans to fire them all."

He lifted a brow. "And how are you going to protect
their pensions?"

"With all the insurance money, investments and such
that Dad left me, as well as the trust fund established
for me by my grandparents."

Sloan stared at her. Did she not know that doing such
a thing might take care of her employees but could leave
her penniless? Sloan leaned forward in the chair and
tried to fight back his anger that Martin Longshire had
placed her in such a predicament. "Like I said, Leslie,
the reason I'm here is because I want to help, and I believe that I can."

She lifted an eyebrow. "How?"

"By coming on as your business partner."

* * *

Leslie was sure she had not heard Sloan correctly. "My business partner?"

"Yes. By doing so, I'll provide you with unlimited resources to continue doing what you need to keep your business operational. As you've indicated, because of Longshire, most of the major banks have put a freeze on loaning you any money."

"And?"

"Well, they wouldn't dare do that with me as your partner. If anything, my investment will let them know your company is financially sound."

"But Mr. Longshire has launched a hostile takeover, Sloan. How can you stop him?"

Sloan's lips thinned in anger. "Stopping him isn't as hard to do as you think. Longshire has been so busy trying to take over your company that he's neglected to protect his own."

"Meaning?"

"He's left his own company vulnerable to another hostile takeover. I have no problem adding Longshire Industries to my portfolio of assets, and I plan to let him know that."

Leslie sat up straight in her chair. "You would take over his company?"

"In a heartbeat if I have to, but I don't feel it's necessary. All I need to do is make sure he knows that I can."

She stared at him, remembering the conversation she'd had with Keosha after Sloan had left the wedding celebration. From what Keosha told her, Sloan was even wealthier than Leslie had thought. In addition to being an executive in his family's business, he had a stake in several business ventures, including his brother Cash's dude ranch in Wyoming, a horse-breeding business with some newfound cousins living in Denver, a security company with some more cousins in Montana and North Carolina, and a film production company in Los Angeles. All of which were doing quite well. That meant Sloan had the financial means to do what he'd suggested. However, she needed to know why, after all these years, he would want to step in and help save her company. Also, she wasn't sure if she could afford him as a business partner. How much of a percentage would he want? Seventy-five percent of her company? Even more than that?

"How much?" she asked him.

He raised a brow. "How much what?"

"What are the partnership terms? Specifically, the percentages?"

Sloan held her gaze. "Seventy-five/twenty-five."

So, he did want seventy-five percent of her company? That meant her company would literally become his. "Are those terms negotiable, Sloan?"

He gave her questioning look. "I think those terms are more than fair. You get seventy-five percent and I get twenty-five percent."

Leslie's mouth nearly dropped open in shock. "Not the other way around?"

"No. And the partnership is only in effect for a year, granted Longshire is no longer a threat. After that time, I will remove myself as your partner and the company will again be yours, free and clear."

Leslie tried to wrap her mind around Sloan's offer. What he was proposing was too good to be true. But she couldn't get all giddy just yet. She had a feeling there was a catch. There had to be. Anything that sounded too good to be true usually was.

That made her ask, "What's the catch, Sloan?"

"What do you mean?"

Oh, he knew just what she meant. It might have been years, but she could still recognize certain Sloan Outlaw habits. Like the way he would flex his fingers when he was up to something. And usually it was something he knew would not make her happy.

"I mean what's in this for you other than a measly twenty-five percent?"

He stopped flexing his fingers and leaned forward in his chair as if to make sure he had her complete attention. The gesture was wasted, because he'd had it from the moment he had walked into her office, wearing a tailor-made business suit and looking the epitome of a wealthy businessman right off the cover of *GQ* magazine.

"There's not a catch, Leslie, but there is a proposition. It's an agreement between us that won't appear in any of the documents, but one you must agree to. I will take your word for it."

"And just what is this agreement?"

"An assurance that I will get what I want for Christmas."

There was something about the way he was looking

at her that made the pulse flutter in her throat. "And what exactly is it that you want for Christmas, Sloan?"

"You, Leslie. I want you for Christmas. In my bed."

Four

Sloan knew what he'd just said had probably shocked her, but she should know just how straightforward he was known to be. While she was sitting there, staring at him as if she thought he'd lost his mind, he decided to say, "After seeing you at the wedding celebration, it quickly became apparent that even after ten years, I'm still attracted to you. Then I remembered that you owed me something."

That got her to talking. "I owe you what?"

"A week. If you recall, you left town at the beginning of spring break, after we'd made plans to spend that week together at my family's cabin on Kodiak Island. It would have been our last time together by ourselves before graduation." He had been scheduled to graduate from college in a few months, although she'd had another two years to go.

What he wouldn't tell her was that he'd intended to give her an engagement ring that week. There was no way he would have graduated, leaving her behind at the university, without putting a ring on her finger. Leslie was a beauty, and too many guys would have been all over her the moment he'd left campus. The thought of waiting two years for them to marry hadn't bothered him, just as long as she'd known how much he loved her and that they were promised to each other.

However, that never happened, because she hadn't shown up on Kodiak Island. He had waited for an entire day at the only airstrip on Kodiak. Then he'd gotten the email telling him to go to hell and that she didn't want to ever see or talk to him again. He had tried calling, but it had gone straight to voice mail.

It had taken him an entire day to get off the island due to a massive rainstorm, but he'd left the moment he could and headed to Anchorage. Once he'd reached her apartment, it was Sarah who'd told him Leslie had packed up and left. She'd then happily told him why. If she couldn't have him, then Leslie wouldn't, either.

Sloan had contacted Leslie's father, who'd told him he had to honor his daughter's wishes and could not tell Sloan where she'd gone. However, Mr. Cassidy did tell him it was somewhere in the lower forty-eight.

Sloan had returned to Kodiak and spent the week alone, drinking booze and regretting the day he'd allowed Leslie into his heart. It had been Garth who'd found him in that pitiful state and talked some sense

into him. His oldest brother reminded him that he had
months before graduation, and that's what he needed
to focus on. Afterward, he'd promised to help Sloan
find Leslie, even if he had to hire a private investigator to do so.

By the time Sloan had graduated, Garth was ready
to keep his end of the bargain by hiring a PI. However,
by then Sloan's heart had hardened. He refused to love
a woman who had not trusted him. So instead of wasting time and money looking for Leslie, he returned to
Fairbanks and began working at his family's business,
determined to forget her and pledging never to give his
heart to another woman again.

"What you're suggesting doesn't make sense, Sloan!"

Her sharp words snapped him out of his reverie. He
needed to leave. All those memories were getting to
him. Standing, he said, "That's your opinion, Leslie. I
suggest you think carefully about your options. When
you do, I'm sure you'll discover the one I'm offering
isn't so bad."

He placed his business card on her desk. "You've got
until noon tomorrow to decide."

Sloan turned and walked out of her office.

Several hours later, an angry Leslie paced her apartment floor while she talked on the phone to Carmen.
"Can you believe the nerve of Sloan Outlaw? Just who
does he think he is?"

"Um, he sounds like a man who wants you for
Christmas."

Leslie stopped pacing. "This isn't funny, Carmen."

"And you don't hear me laughing. I wish some man who looked like Sloan wanted me for Christmas. I would wrap myself up to be put under his tree anytime. Then I would wait patiently for him to unwrap me."

Leslie rolled her eyes. "Will you stop being a romantic for once?"

"No. Someone is offering you a chance to actually live the life while I'm just dealing with fantasies."

"Listen, Carmen, the man wants me in his bed."

"So? It's not like you've never been there before."

Leslie dropped down on the sofa. "Those times were different. We were in love then. We aren't now. All he wants is revenge for what I did to him ten years ago. That makes him no better than Martin Longshire."

"Isn't he? Mr. Longshire wants to destroy your company. Sounds to me like Sloan Outlaw is trying to help you save it. Think about it, Les. He's offering you a temporary partnership that even you said was too good to be true. All you have to do is something you probably want to do anyway."

"Carmen!"

"Just keeping it real. Are you going to try and convince me that you haven't once wondered if he's still good in bed? And according to you, he was good. 'Testosterone on legs' is how you described him to me, and he's all you used to talk about. In fact, you admitted he's the reason you never could sleep with another guy, because he'd spoiled you for anyone else. I bet he doesn't know you haven't slept with another guy since him."

Leslie frowned. "That is none of his business."

"True, but I still say being his Christmas present

would be your present, too. It's either enjoy his bed or lose your company. For me it's a no-brainer."

Leslie thought about everything Carmen had said. She glanced at her watch, knowing she needed to jump on a call with her company's attorney. "I need to go, Carmen. My attorney will be calling in a few minutes."

"When do you give Sloan your decision?"

"By noon tomorrow."

"Okay. I know after sleeping on it you'll wake up tomorrow and make the right one."

She knew in Carmen's mind, the right one was agreeing to Sloan's proposal. "I'll talk to you later, Carm."

"Okay, but just so you know, Sloan's offer pretty much sounds like that Christmas miracle you mentioned you've been hoping for. Bye, Les."

Later that night, while Leslie lay in bed, all kinds of thoughts were going through her mind. According to the phone call she'd had with Stan, the bank would not give her the extension on the loan. That left her with no options on the table other than Sloan's.

Like Carmen, her attorney thought Sloan's offer was a godsend, almost too good to be true, and that made Stan suspicious of Sloan's motives. Of course, she didn't tell Stan about the condition Sloan had attached to his proposal. However, to arrest Stan's concerns, she explained that she and Sloan had dated in college and what he was doing was a favor. That had satisfied Stan, and he'd even said she was lucky to have a friend who would come to her aid.

Such a friend…

She had known the old Sloan, the one who didn't

have a ruthless bone in his body. Granted, the Sloan Outlaw who'd shown up at her office today still had charm and impeccable manners, but she knew he'd changed. And so had she. Considering how they had broken up and the lies she had believed about him, she was surprised he was willing to help her at all. And why would he want them to sleep together, of all things? To her, it didn't make sense, because they'd always made love and not just had sex. To them, there had always been a difference. Evidently, he thought that now there wasn't a difference.

But still, she needed to talk to him, because there were questions that needed answering before she could make a final decision.

Easing out of bed, she pulled his business card out of her purse. It was just a little past ten, but he used to be a night owl. Was he still? Was he even in Wasilla or had he gone back to Fairbanks? She would find out soon enough, she thought, as she punched in his number.

"Hello?"

"Sloan, this is Leslie."

"Yes, Leslie?"

She swallowed deeply. He still had a sexy phone voice. "There are a few things I need to know about your proposal before I can make a decision."

"What do you need to know?"

She nibbled on her bottom lip. "It's about my week at your cabin, if I decide to do it."

"What about it?"

"Will we sleep together just one time?"

"Would we have slept together just one time ten years ago, Leslie?" was his quick comeback.

She frowned. "Things were different then, Sloan."

"I'm aware of that. What I want is the week I didn't get. I would not have forced myself on you then, and I won't do it now. I will leave it up to you if or when we make love."

"Oh?" She was surprised to hear that. "And what if I decide that I don't want to make love to you at all during that week?"

She heard his soft chuckle, and it sent warm shivers through her body. "I'm not worried about that happening."

"I'm not the same person, Sloan."

"Neither am I. We might find it interesting to discover what those differences are."

"Are you still in Wasilla?"

"Yes. I plan to be in town until you make a decision. If you accept my proposal, then I need to hang around to make sure Longshire knows I mean business." He paused. "I know your company shuts down for Christmas this Friday. I'd like you ready to go to the cabin with me the following weekend. We'll stay for a week."

She frowned. "What if I've made plans for that week? What if I have a boyfriend?"

"Have you? Do you?"

As much as she now wished she could say yes to both questions, she truthfully couldn't. "No, I'm not dating seriously at the moment, and as far as my plans for the holidays—"

She paused when she felt the thickness in her throat.

She tried not to think about the fact that this Christmas she would be all alone. "With Dad gone, I didn't have any plans," she finally said. Then to change the subject, she asked, "What about your job?"

"What about it?" he countered.

"Don't you have to go to work?"

"No. My vacation started the first of December. I'm off until after New Year's."

"I see."

"Any more questions?"

"Yes. Will you involve yourself in the day-to-day operations of the company?"

"No. There's no reason that I should. Handle your business just as you would if I wasn't involved. And just so you know, the twenty-five percent that I would get will be going directly to my charities."

That was another surprise. Drawing in a deep breath, she said, "I'll call you tomorrow with my decision. I need to sleep on it. Good night, Sloan."

"Good night, Leslie. Pleasant dreams."

She quickly hung up. Saying "pleasant dreams" was how he would always end their calls at night, because he'd known her dreams would always be of him…and they would always be pleasant. Did he assume that now? Putting her cell phone back on the nightstand, she snuggled under the warm covers.

What bothered her more than anything was knowing she *would* have pleasant dreams of him tonight. How could she not when Carmen and Stan were right? Sloan had become her Christmas miracle. With that thought in mind, she settled in bed and closed her eyes. The reality of the situation was that Sloan Outlaw was back in her life, and she honestly wasn't sure how she felt about it.

The next morning Sloan woke up around seven, showered and got dressed while thinking about his conversation with Leslie last night. After the call had ended, he'd tried turning his attention back to the murder mystery he'd been watching on television but found that he couldn't. He'd always thought she had a sexy voice. This older Leslie's voice was even sexier, which pretty much agreed with the rest of her.

He had tried not to let it annoy him that she had to sleep on his offer. Although she had apologized and admitted she now knew Sarah had lied, he couldn't get past the fact that she had believed her roommate in the first place. Was that why she was having a problem trusting him now? Even with his generous terms, did she think he wanted to take her company? If she did, then she'd classed him in the same category as Longshire.

Sloan hadn't wanted to take Leslie's actions personally. Any competent businessperson knew not to make hasty decisions. She was merely following the rules, and he would expect the same of anyone he did business with. But then, he'd never intended to sleep with any of his business associates. That made this entire situation with Leslie different.

He'd meant what he'd told her last night. He had never forced himself on her before, and he wouldn't be doing it now. However, if she thought they could stay together at the cabin and not share a bed, then she would only be fooling herself. Whenever they were alone for any period of time, they were spontaneous combustion just waiting to explode.

Although they'd been apart for ten years, he'd picked up on the strong sexual attraction between them at the wedding reception. Even Redford said he'd noticed it from across the room, which was why he hadn't come back to join them when he'd seen them talking.

Sloan had picked up those same vibes yesterday in her office. Even when they had been discussing something as important as the possibility of her losing her company, whenever their eyes met, desire had flowed between them—whether they wanted it to or not.

There was no doubt in his mind it had been a mutual attraction both times. For that reason, he could understand her call last night to clarify a few things. She of all people knew what potent sexual beings they used to be and still were.

And why he had held his breath at the possibility that she was seriously involved with someone. Although after intense questioning, Redford had said he'd not heard she was dating anyone. But still, Redford's information might have been wrong. Would it have mattered? Yes, it would have. Unlike Redford, Sloan had never encroached on another man's territory, and he didn't intend to start now.

He was about to leave his hotel room for breakfast when his cell phone rang. Before going to bed, he had added Leslie's phone number to his contact list and had even given her a special ringtone. He didn't want to analyze the reason he'd done that.

He clicked on the phone. "Yes, Leslie?" He immediately wished he could bite off his tongue. Now she knew he had her name in his phone.

"I've made a decision, Sloan."

He paused a moment. "And what is your decision?"

"That you and I become temporary business partners."

Why was he releasing a relieved breath? He didn't want to admit that the alternative was one he would not have been able to accept. The only reason he had gotten involved was because he refused to let a man like Martin Longshire think he could get away with being a bully.

"Okay. We need to meet tonight and plan our strategy. Let's do dinner at six."

"Dinner?"

"Yes, dinner. You know, that meal people usually eat at the end of the day."

"Yes, smart-ass, I know it."

Sloan couldn't help but chuckle. Now this was the Leslie he knew. The one who could hold her own against anyone, including him. He had a feeling Martin Longshire had begun breaking her down when she hadn't been able to see a way out. Now Sloan was giving her one and she could go back to being herself again. The woman he used to...

He blinked, knowing he couldn't go there. He would never go there with her again. "Okay, since you know what it is, will you be free at six?"

"Yes, but why wait until then? You can come to my office at five."

"No, I can't. There's a business call I need to be on at four."

"I thought you were off work from Outlaw Freight Lines for the rest of December."

Was she questioning him? Would there always be an issue of trust between them? "The meeting has nothing to do with Outlaw Freight Lines. Will you be able to do dinner or not?" he snapped.

"Yes, just tell me where to meet you," she said in a brusque tone.

"My hotel."

"Excuse me?"

Sloan rubbed the back of his neck, getting more agitated by the second. "I said my hotel, Leslie, not my hotel room. There happens to be a nice restaurant, the Elderbrae, located in the Ghanis Hotel."

"I know where it is. In fact, it's right around the corner from where I live."

He'd known that from his research and had chosen his hotel for that very reason. "In that case, there won't be a problem in you finding it," he said.

"No problem at all."

"Good. I'll see you at six."

Five

Leslie walked into the Ghanis Hotel and glanced around. She shouldn't have been surprised that Sloan was staying at the most elegant hotel in Wasilla or that he would want to dine at one of the most exclusive restaurants. She had dined at the Elderbrae a few times with her father, who claimed nobody could cook a steak to perfection like they could.

Pausing, she took in the hotel's Christmas decorations. A huge Christmas tree stood in the middle of the lobby. It had to be at least twenty feet tall, was beautifully decorated and surrounded by more than a hundred beautiful red poinsettias. On both sides of the ring of poinsettias were life-size polar bears on their hind legs. The bears looked so real she instinctively took a step back.

"I promise they won't bite."

Looking over her shoulder, she saw Sloan was walking toward her. She then glanced back at the display. "They look so real."

"Yes, they do. I saw them when I checked in and wondered if it would be safe to stay here."

His comment made her laugh, because if anyone should be used to bears it was Sloan. His family owned that cabin on Kodiak Island, and everyone knew there were more bears on that island than people. Not polar bears but grizzlies, and they were the worst kind.

"I've only heard good things about the food served here, so I hope you're hungry," he said as they headed over to the restaurant.

"Whatever you heard is true. Dad and I ate here a few times, and the food was fantastic."

When they reached the entrance, they were met by the smiling maître d'. Within minutes they were shown to their table that provided a picturesque view of snow-capped mountains. She knew tables on this side of the restaurant went for a premium, but the view was worth it. "That view is beautiful," she finally said, glancing over at him.

"I think so, too," he said, looking at her. He hadn't been looking out the window when he'd said it, but she dismissed the possibility they were talking about different views.

"I'm surprised you're not staying in Anchorage since it's only a short drive away."

He chuckled. "I had no desire to drive the forty

minutes back and forth when my business is here in Wasilla."

His business? Did he think of the situation involving her as "his business"? A part of her should have been glad he did, even if it sounded so impersonal.

At that moment a waitress appeared to take their drink order and presented them with menus. When she left, Leslie looked up from her menu to find Sloan staring at her. Lifting a brow, she asked, "Is anything wrong?"

He smiled, and she wished he hadn't. Sloan Outlaw had the kind of smile that could make a woman weak in the knees even while they were already sitting down.

"I was just noticing that you haven't changed much."

If he thought that, then he was wrong. "Of course I've changed, Sloan."

Although he might be referring to physical appearance, she was referring to her emotions. Leaving school in Anchorage the way she had and dealing with pain and heartbreak for nearly seven years had broken her. And then to discover it had all been a lie, and for Sarah to have the nerve to gloat about it in front of others, had been another kind of pain within itself. Probably the worst thing to ever happen to her.

No, losing Sloan because of that lie was the worst thing to ever happen to her.

"I've grown an inch taller, Sloan," she said proudly. "You probably can't tell since I'm always in heels."

"Trust me, Leslie. I've noticed all your changes."

It wasn't what he'd said but how he'd said it, in a low and intimate voice that gave her pause. They needed to change the subject, and she decided to take the initiative to do it. "So, Garth and Cash are both married now?"

A genuine smile touched his lips. "Yes. I'm sure you remember Garth's wife, Regan. Her father had been our company's pilot for years."

"Yes, of course I remember Regan. I met her when I visited your family one Christmas. I liked Regan."

"Well, she and Garth got married. Cash fell in love with someone he met when he went to Wyoming for the reading of his mother's will. He and his wife, Brianna, live in Wyoming. She's pregnant and having twins in a couple of months."

"Twins? Wow! That's great."

"We all think so, too. Cash will make a wonderful father."

"I can't believe he moved from Alaska."

"I know, and that took getting used to. But he loves the huge spread he inherited there, and I've never seen him happier."

"Does he still work for the company?"

"Yes, he operates a satellite office on his ranch."

At that moment the waitress returned to take their order, and they both decided to try the steak. "You still like your steak burned, I see," he said when the waitress walked off.

She smiled over at him and said, "And you still prefer yours half-cooked."

"Some things never change."

She took a sip of her wine while thinking that most things did. "So, Sloan, now that I've agreed for you to become my business partner, what is your plan regarding Longshire?" No need to beat around the bush when his whole purpose for taking her to dinner tonight was to discuss business.

"The plans are already in place. By midnight he'll know things are not going as he expected, and he'll be quite upset about it. If he shows up unannounced, I suggest you have security escort him off the premises."

Leslie nodded as she studied Sloan. She had a feeling there was something he hadn't told her. "Is there anything else I should know about?"

Sloan leaned back in his chair. "To let him know I meant business, I took one of his companies from him."

Leslie nearly choked on her drink. "You took his company?"

"Not his major company, Leslie. It was a company he took over last month. I happened to find out about them when I did research on what he was doing to your company. Like your father, he had some kind personal vendetta against the family. Evidently Longshire is a man who holds grudges."

"What kind of company is it?" she asked.

"It's a family business that's been around for generations. It's run by an older couple and their offspring. All toy makers."

"Toy makers?"

"Yes. I understand that for years they'd been quite successful, but for the past year, sales had been declining, and then they were dropped by their distributor. I discovered all of it was Longshire's doing, just to get back at the family."

"Why on earth would Longshire need a toy manu-facturing company?"

"He doesn't. Just like he doesn't need a cosmetics company. He's doing it because he knows he can, and he evidently likes to make people's lives a living hell. Like I said, he holds grudges."

"What an ass."

"Yes, and the sad thing is that he has no plans for the company. He just wants to ruin it. After doing my research, I decided that in the right hands the toy mak-ing company would be a good investment. The first thing I plan to do is hire the family back and put them in charge. It would boost their local economy."

She nodded. What Sloan hadn't said, but what she'd figured, knowing Sloan like she did, was that unlike Longshire, he would sell that family back their com-pany once he'd made it financially sound for them. Les-lie took a sip of her wine and said, "Longshire is going to get even more upset when he finds out you're giving that family back their company."

Sloan lifted a brow. "What makes you think I'll be giving that family their company back?"

Leslie shrugged. "A hunch." When he didn't say whether her hunch was right or not, she asked, "Where's this place? Is it here in Wasilla?"

"No. The North Pole."

"North Pole, Alaska?"

"Yes."

Leslie chuckled. "An older couple whose family makes toys in North Pole, Alaska. That's interesting."

He smiled. "I think it's interesting as well. I plan to fly there to meet them this weekend."

"You've told me what to expect of Martin Longshire, Sloan. Now I need to know what to expect of you."

Sloan glanced up from his meal and met Leslie's direct gaze. Instead of answering her, he pointed to her glass. "Need more wine?"

She frowned, and he thought she looked cute when she did so. "Why? Is that your way of saying what you're about to tell me will make me want a drink?"

He chuckled. "No. I just noticed your glass was half-full."

She nodded. "Thanks for your concern, but I'm fine. Now, if you will please answer my question."

Sloan shrugged. "There's really nothing else to tell you, Leslie. I think I made it clear yesterday what my expectations are. I want you for Christmas. Why are we having this discussion, anyway? You agreed to my terms."

"Yes, but I need you to clarify a few things."

"Things like what?" he asked, cutting into his steak.

"What do you have planned for us that week?"

"Other than hoping we make love every day, every hour, using every position known to man and then some that few men know about yet?" Sloan knew he had, for the second day in a row, shocked Leslie speechless.

"You're basing your agenda for that week on the assumption I will fall at your feet."

"No, I'm basing my agenda on the assumption that you'll share my bed." He drew in a deep breath. "Look,

Leslie, we can hash and rehash the issue all we want, but it won't get us anywhere. You have your mind made up about not sleeping with me, and I have my mind made up that you will. Let's just see how things turn out. However, the one thing you need to do is trust me."

"Trust you?"

"Yes. There was a time you trusted me, but then, through no fault of mine, you stopped."

Her spine stiffened. "How can I trust a man who has told me he wants me in his bed?"

"There was a time you appreciated my honesty. Would you prefer I not tell you?"

"I prefer you not to want *me* for Christmas."

That made him ask, "What is it that you want for Christmas, Leslie?" He couldn't help being curious. Now she was nibbling on her bottom lip in a way that had blood rushing straight down to his groin.

She stared into her drink instead of at him when she said, "I haven't thought about Christmas much, Sloan, since it will be my first without Dad. We would always spend the holidays together. The only exception was that year I spent Christmas with you and your family."

Leslie then looked up at him, and that's when he saw it. The deep sadness in her eyes. "Even while I lived in DC, Dad would either come there to spend the holidays with me and Aunt Ella, or I would come home here. With Aunt Ella and Dad both deceased, this will be my first Christmas alone. So the only thing I want for Christmas will be the ability to get through the day."

Sloan didn't say anything as he took a sip of his drink. He recalled the holidays only had come to mean a lot to him because of her. Christmas had been her favorite holiday, and she'd let everyone in her inner circle know it. For him, his brothers and sister, it hadn't had the same meaning.

The Outlaws had discovered their differences when Sloan had taken Leslie home with him during their college holiday break. First, she'd been aghast that they had not planned to put up a tree or any decorations. It didn't take long for her to whip the Outlaws—Bart excluded—into shape. By Christmas Eve they had gone out and bought a live Christmas tree and had it decorated with newly purchased ornaments. She had been a novelty, and his family had fallen in love with her immediately. After her visit, the Outlaws never failed to put up a Christmas tree again.

The thought of her spending time alone on Christmas bothered him. After their week at the cabin, what would she do for those remaining days before Christmas? What about the week after Christmas that led into the New Year? He shouldn't care, but he did.

He could invite Leslie to spend Christmas with his family this year. As they'd done for the past few years, the Outlaws would spend the holidays in Denver with their cousins the Westmorelands. They would remain through New Year's Day, since the annual Westmoreland charity ball would be held on New Year's Eve.

However, a part of him didn't want to include her in his life that way. He didn't want to give his siblings any ideas that there was more than a business arrangement between them. But there was another part of him that could not forget their history and didn't want her to spend the holidays alone.

Six

The next day, Leslie looked up from the document on her desk upon hearing the commotion outside her office door. Stiffening, she recognized one of the voices just seconds before her office door flew open and Martin Longshire stood there. Anger radiated not just from his features but also his stance.

"You won't get away with this," he snarled. "You're a fool if you think an ex-boyfriend can save your company."

She wondered how he knew about her and Sloan's past relationship. Standing, she crossed her arms over her chest, but before she could say anything, Beverly moved from behind him and asked, "Do you want me to call security, Ms. Cassidy?"

Leslie switched her gaze from Longshire to Beverly. "If he hasn't left in five minutes, then yes, call security."

Beverly glanced over at Longshire with an expression as if she wasn't convinced leaving Leslie with him would be a good thing to do.

"I'll be fine, Beverly. Five minutes and he will be gone."

"Like hell I will!"

Ignoring the man's outburst, Leslie said, "Five minutes, Beverly. If it makes you feel better, alert security to be on standby just in case."

Beverly smiled and said, "I think that's a good idea." She then swept past Longshire to leave but left the door open. Like before, he slammed it shut, but at least he hadn't given Beverly a smart-alecky remark like he had the last time.

Leslie turned her attention back to Longshire. "State your business and leave. Now you have four minutes."

He strode over to her desk, and for a minute she thought he would reach out and grab her, but he didn't. Instead, he said, "You've made a mistake by bringing Sloan Outlaw into this. And he's made a mistake by taking one of my companies from me. Neither you nor Outlaw will get away with it. Now I will destroy you both."

Longshire then turned and walked out of the office. When he'd opened the door, Leslie had seen two members of her security team standing by Beverly's desk to escort him out of the building.

She drew in a deep breath as she sat back down in her chair. Beverly stood in the doorway. "Are you all right?"

Leslie nodded. "Yes, I'm fine."

Moments after Beverly left, she pulled her phone from her purse to call Sloan. Before they parted ways after dinner last night, he had told her to call him if Longshire showed up today.

"Yes, Leslie?"

She felt an intense pull in her stomach at the sound of him saying her name. Last night over dinner, although they'd disagreed on a number of things, the physical attraction between them had been mind-boggling. "Martin Longshire just left, and he made threats."

"Against you?" Leslie could hear the anger in his voice.

"Against both of us, Sloan. He said he will destroy us both. Something else he said surprised me."

"What?"

"He knew you were my ex-boyfriend."

"Um, I wonder how he knows that?"

"I'm not sure," she said. "I guess he did research after wondering why you'd come to my aid the way you did."

"Doesn't matter. He's gotten the message that he's wasting his time trying to take away your company."

"How long will you be in town?" she asked him.

"I'm flying out Saturday."

"Oh." She wondered why hearing that he was leaving Wasilla was somewhat of a downer.

"Cassidy Cosmetics closes for the holidays on Friday, right?" he then asked her.

"Yes, why?"

"How would you like to fly to North Pole with me to meet those toy makers?"

Leslie lifted a brow. "You want me to go with you?"

"Why not? I'm only going to be there a couple of days. And before you get bent out of shape, let me go on record to say I will make sure we get separate rooms at the hotel. I recall you've never been...unless that has changed over the last ten years."

"No, I've never been to North Pole."

"You've always wanted to do so, now here's your chance, Leslie. Of course, if you don't trust yourself around me, then I understand."

She frowned. "I do trust myself around you, Sloan."

"Does that mean you'll go?"

Leslie recalled when they'd met, he couldn't believe she had never visited North Pole. He'd figured every Alaskan had done so at some time during their childhood. She had explained that although she'd always wanted to go, there was never time to do so. Her parents had worked long days making the company a success, and they rarely traveled too far from Wasilla. Now Sloan was giving her a chance to go there. With him. Should she?

Why not? Hadn't she just told him that she trusted herself around him? What they'd once shared was over. She'd blown things years ago, and they'd both moved on. Besides, wouldn't they be spending a week together at his cabin in a week or so anyway? "Yes, Sloan, I would love to go. Thanks for inviting me."

"I'll pick you up Saturday morning at six."

"All right. You'll need my address. I'm no longer living in my father's house. I sold it."

"I know where you live now."

Leslie frowned, bothered that it seemed both Sloan and Martin Longshire knew too much about her.

"You're up early, Sloan."

Sloan chuckled as he walked out of the hotel to his rental car. "I'm on my way somewhere, Cole."

Sloan's cousin Cole Westmoreland was a former Texas Ranger who had married Dr. Patrina Foreman. The couple lived in Montana and had three kids. When Cole retired as a ranger, he joined forces with another cousin, Quade Westmoreland, who'd worked for a special services unit to protect the president, to start a network of security companies.

"So where are you headed?" Cole asked.

"The North Pole."

"You're kidding, right?"

"Nope," Sloan said as he loaded his luggage into the trunk of his car. "I bought a toy company there."

"Yeah, right. The next thing you're going to tell me is that it's run by an older couple named the Kringles."

Sloan smiled. "It's run by an older couple, but their last name is Yule."

"Whatever."

Sloan shook his head, knowing his cousin probably didn't believe him. There was no need to tell him the man's first name was Rudolph. "The reason I'm calling is because I have a job for you."

"What?"

"There's a person I want you to investigate by the name of Martin Longshire."

"Anything in particular I need to look for?" Cole wanted to know.

"Not sure. I screwed up his plans to take over a couple of companies, and he's known for getting revenge. I want to be ready if he tries."

"I'll dig to see if there's something in his past we could use as leverage if it comes to that."

"I'm sure if there's something out there on Longshire, you'll find it. You're good at what you do."

Cole laughed. "If you have so much confidence in my abilities, then let me take a crack at finding out why your old man refuses to claim the Westmorelands as kin. That's rubbish when you can't deny these strong Westmoreland genes."

Sloan knew that was the truth. Not only did all the male Westmorelands look alike and favor the male Outlaws, but their cousin Bailey and his sister, Charm, looked similar as well. "Charm's mother, Claudia, persuaded us to not look into it. She felt it was an invasion of Dad's privacy and felt when he got ready to tell us why he was so opposed, then he would."

Sloan and his brothers had agreed not to let their father's refusal to accept their Westmoreland kin have any bearing on their willingness to do so. Over the past years, the Westmoreland and Outlaw cousins had formed a close bond.

"Will you be flying that toy plane of yours to North Pole?" Cole asked.

He chuckled. "Yes, one day I'll let you at the wheel."

Sloan knew Cole had his pilot's license. In addition to the security company, Cole owned a helicopter service that provided transportation between the various mountains in Bozeman, Montana, to the people who lived on them. Cole's father was one such person who lived on a huge mountain they called Corey's Mountain.

After disconnecting the call, Sloan thought about the woman he would be seeing in a few minutes. The same one who'd occupied his thoughts most of the night. He was trying to keep a level head where Leslie Cassidy was concerned. Once burned, you never wanted to experience such pain again. However, the thought of her being alone for the holidays was outweighing any desire to keep his distance.

Sloan couldn't imagine such loneliness, because he'd always had his siblings. They all knew, although Bart would never admit it, that their father had loved having a full house, and they'd been content living on the Outlaw compound. However, when they got older and Bart began trying to manipulate them, they'd each moved into their own places. All except for Charm. She adored the old man and managed to see past his faults. Besides, like her mother, Claudia, Charm knew how to handle Bart.

Pulling into Leslie's yard, Sloan saw that even more snow had fallen overnight in the area where she lived. He hoped there wouldn't be a delay in getting his plane off the ground.

Flexing his gloved hands a few times and tightening the scarf around his neck, he got out of the car. There was no way you could live in Alaska and not be used to the cold and snow. To them it was a way of life, but as far as he was concerned there was no other place he'd rather live. He had traveled to most of the states in the lower forty-eight, and although some had been nice to visit, there was no place like Alaska.

As he shoved his hands into the pockets of his long coat, he glanced around. There had to be at least three feet of snow, possibly more. But it was beautiful.

Sloan liked Leslie's home. It sat in a cul-de-sac with four others, all spaced a nice distance apart. He was glad she hadn't asked how he'd known where she lived. Had she done so, he would have had to confess to researching any personal information he could find.

She had moved out of her father's house a month after he'd passed away. Sloan recalled the house had been massive, much too large for one person. The size of this house was perfect for her.

He also gathered from his research that since returning to Alaska, she had rolled up her sleeves and worked hard beside her father. The bulk of Cassidy Cosmetics business was in Alaska. The businessman in him wondered why Lester Cassidy never expanded into the lower forty-eight.

Ringing her doorbell, Sloan was surprised when she opened the door immediately. His gaze automatically moved over her from head to toe. Why had he forgotten how beautiful she could look first thing in the morning? He was suddenly filled with a hefty dose of desire. To a degree he didn't want or need.

"Good morning, Sloan. Come on in. I just need to grab my travel bag and coat," she said, walking off.

Sloan nodded, unable to do anything other than that.

She wore a pair of skinny burgundy corduroy pants, a light gray pullover sweater and knee-high black boots.

Leslie had such a gorgeous body, he couldn't help but stand in the doorway and stare. Just watching her ass in motion was an arousal waiting to happen, and seeing her small waist and all those curves had him transfixed.

Glancing back over her shoulder, she stopped and turned back around, a questioning look on her face. "Is anything wrong?"

He drew in a deep breath and decided to play dumb. "What makes you think something is wrong?"

She shoved her hands in the pockets of her pants. "You're standing there with the door wide-open, letting out the heat."

"Oh," he said, entering her home and quickly closing the door behind him.

When she continued walking toward an area that he figured was her bedroom, he glanced around, not wanting to think about where she slept. She had decorated for the holidays and had a nice tree. He moved closer as an ornament caught his attention. It was the same one he'd given her years ago. He was surprised she still had it.

"I'm ready."

Sloan turned around. He'd forgotten how she dressed warmly from her head to her toes. Cold Alaska weather was never going to get the best of her. She looked cute in her fur hat and knitted face mask with a scarf to match. Then there was her heavy wool coat. There was no doubt in his mind it was totally lined.

"Okay, let's go," he said, taking her overnight bag.

Seven

"You can stop holding your breath now, Leslie."

She glanced over at Sloan and couldn't hold back her chuckle. She'd never liked small planes, and although he knew how to operate one, she couldn't help the nervousness floating around in her stomach.

He'd told her years ago that the Outlaws' corporate pilot had taught them all to fly. Now Sloan had his personal plane, a Cessna, and according to him it took him wherever he needed to go in the United States.

"It wasn't snowing when we took off, but it is now," she said.

"It's light, and this baby can handle it."

Why at that moment did she recall him saying that same thing to her the first time they'd made love? She had been a virgin, and the moment she'd seen him without clothes—especially that part below the waist—her expression must have said it all. He'd strolled over to her with his sexy walk, touched her between the legs and said, "This baby can handle it."

"Leslie?"

She glanced over at him. "Yes?"

"I asked if you slept well last night."

Leslie figured he'd asked the question while her mind had been preoccupied with memories from the past. "Yes. It was the best sleep I've had since Dad died. It felt good knowing my company won't be taken from me. I'm grateful to you for making that possible."

"I don't want your gratitude, Leslie."

She didn't say anything, because she knew what he wanted. He'd told her plainly. He wanted her…for Christmas…in his bed. Deciding to change the subject, she said, "Is it true your family located relatives you didn't know you had in the lower forty-eight?"

He glanced over at her. "Who told you that?"

There was no way she would tell him that Keosha had told her. Then he would know she'd asked about him. So she said, "I think during one of our conversations you mentioned it."

He nodded. "Yes, but we didn't find them, they found us. The Westmorelands had evidence leading them to believe their great-grandfather Raphael Westmoreland fathered an illegitimate child. They hired a private investigator to determine if it was true, and the man's investigation led them right to our doorstep."

"And you're sure they are your kinfolk?"

"You wouldn't ask me that if you'd ever seen us together. We share some strong Westmoreland genes. Practically every Westmoreland has an Outlaw cousin who looks almost identical to them. The resemblance is so uncanny that Cash swapped places with Bane Westmoreland in a government sting operation."

"So, there's a Westmoreland who looks like you?" She couldn't imagine another man having similar sexy features.

"Yes. Derringer Westmoreland. We honestly do favor, but I'm sure you'll be able to tell us apart."

Leslie thought about what he'd said. Had he just hinted there was a chance she would meet his cousin one day? She honestly didn't see that happening. "You've gotten to know these Westmorelands?"

"Yes, and it's the oddest thing. Although we only met around five years ago, we act as if we've known each other all our lives. There are a lot of Westmorelands living in Colorado, Texas, California, Montana, Georgia and North Carolina. You ever heard of Thorn Westmoreland?"

"Of course. He's that celebrity who builds and races motorcycles."

"Yes, and he's a cousin. And do you recall reading a few years back when an American woman married a sheikh from the Middle East?"

"Yes. There was a huge spread about it in several magazines. I believe she was a doctor."

"Well, that was Delaney Westmoreland, Thorn's sister. Now she's a queen, since her husband, Jamal Ari Yasir, has become king. She won't be visiting this year since she's expecting."

"She is?"

"Yes, twins. They have two older kids and waited years before deciding to have any more. I heard they always wanted at least four, so now they will get them."

He paused a moment to move one of the controls. "I also noticed you had a Rock Mason novel on your coffee table."

"Yes, what about it?"

"He's a cousin as well. His real name is Stone Westmoreland."

"Honestly? I went to a Rock Mason book signing at Howard. I still have that autographed book." She then asked, "How does your father feel about all these new relatives?"

"Bart is pretty much in denial. He refuses to believe his grandfather was adopted and claims we're Outlaws and not Westmorelands."

She lifted a brow. "Even after seeing the resemblance in all of you?"

"Yes, even after that. It's the strangest thing how he refuses to accept them as kin. But it doesn't matter if he accepts them or not, because we do."

"There has to be a reason he feels that way."

"Maybe there is and maybe there isn't, or it could be Bart is just being Bart. You've met Dad, and I would tell you all the time how ornery he is. Bart likes controlling every situation, but he can't control this one. My siblings and I are adults who refuse to let Dad tell us what to do."

Sloan chuckled. "Doesn't really matter since most of his time these days is spent courting Claudia."

"Charm's mom?"

"Yes. She's the one woman who refused to marry him."

He reached up to adjust a control near the top. "We'll be landing at the Fairbanks airport in less than thirty minutes."

She knew they would get a rental car from the airport and drive to North Pole. "How far is North Pole from Fairbanks?"

"Twenty minutes. And just so you know, the landing might be a little rough, since there's a lot of snow. The runway has been deiced, so we should be okay."

She glanced over at him and drew in a nervous breath. "Okay, Sloan. I'll take your word for it."

A couple of hours later, Sloan and Leslie had checked into the hotel in North Pole. The landing of the plane was just like he'd warned her it would be, but she hadn't complained. A rental car had been waiting for them, and they'd driven to the only hotel in town.

Just like he'd told Leslie, they had separate rooms; however, his room was next to hers. Her expression had been unreadable when he'd told her they would join the Yules for dinner at five. Other than lifting a brow at the older couple's last name, she merely nodded before entering her hotel room.

Moving over to the window, he looked out with his hands shoved in his pockets. Although a thick blanket of snow covered nearly everything, it was easy to see that North Pole, Alaska—population of a little more than two thousand people—was a beautiful small town. One of his fondest memories was visiting here around the holidays as a kid with his classmates. He recalled the huge gift shop located in Santa's House that had some of the neatest items.

Moving away from the window, he went to his duffel bag to unpack. He was excited to share North Pole with Leslie. And little did she know that having her sitting next to him in the cockpit had placed temptation solidly at his feet. For starters, she had worn that perfume he liked so much. He also noted she liked keeping the conversation going whenever she was nervous about something. He figured what had her anxious had been them flying in bad weather.

Was that the reason he had shared more about his family than he would normally have done to someone who was not a close friend? Granted, she had met everyone years ago and had been considered a close friend of the family then. He didn't consider her one now. However, how should he refer to a woman he'd traveled over three hundred miles to help?

A woman you've been thinking a lot about since running into her again?

Every time he looked at her mouth, he recalled how sweet her lips could be. Whenever he saw her hands, he remembered her touch and how he had taught her to stroke him in certain places. Whenever they'd made love, it had propelled him to a level of ecstasy he'd never been to before and, to be honest, hadn't been to since her.

He had dated a lot of women over the years, but none had come close to fulfilling his needs, wants and fantasies like Leslie. But thanks to her he had learned a valuable lesson—to never give his heart to a woman or she was liable to crush it.

He rubbed his hand down his face. Leslie meant nothing to him now, and he hadn't done any more for her than he would have for someone else in her predicament. The Yules were a prime example of that fact. But on the other hand, he didn't want the Yules for Christmas. He didn't go to bed thinking of them and wake up doing the same thing. It hadn't been the Yules on his mind during the flight here, and his anticipation of five o'clock had nothing to do with meeting the Yules and everything to do with seeing Leslie again.

Every muscle in his body tensed. He had to stop this right now before his attraction to her got out of hand. He had to remember the pain she had caused him when she'd left without a trace. Left because of a lie she had believed. How had she honestly thought he could have betrayed her the way Sarah had claimed? Hadn't his words of love, his actions, proven anything? Obviously not.

He glanced at his watch. He would rest awhile. Hopefully by dinnertime he would have reclaimed complete control of his senses.

"How are things going with you and Sloan?"

Leslie sat on the edge of the bed. "Why do you have to make it sound as if we're a couple, Carmen?"

"A little wishful thinking on my part, maybe."

"Let's not go there."

"Well, you did fly to North Pole with him. I never

knew there was really such a place. I thought it was made up."

Leslie smiled as she got up to walk over to the window. "I'm sure a lot of people think the same thing, but the town does exist. This is where all those letters to Santa end up, which is why their post office is the most popular in the world. I imagine it's pretty busy this time of the year."

"I'm going to add that place to my bucket list."

"You do that, and the next time you come visit me in Alaska, I'll make sure we come here. It's a beautiful little town, and it's so Christmassy. I'm looking out of my hotel window, and it's so picture perfect. Even with all the snow."

"Please take pictures," Carmen begged.

Leslie chuckled. "I will."

"For you as an Alaskan, I'm surprised it's your first time there."

Carmen recalled Sloan had said the same thing when they'd met years ago. He'd teased her and said he would take away her Alaska card. "Dad was always too busy, and the drive to North Pole from Wasilla is over three hundred miles. There was no time. When we did take vacations, we went to check on Aunt Ella."

"And just think, it's your first time and you're doing it with Sloan."

Leslie frowned. "You're trying to make us into a couple again, Carm."

"I can't help it. How did your employees react when you told them you wouldn't be losing the company?"

"They were happy. Some have worked for my parents since the time they started this company over thirty years ago."

"I'm glad things turned out the way they did, Leslie. You should be forever grateful to Sloan."

"And I will be. Can we change the subject?"

"I thought we had. Not my fault that all the talking points, regardless of the conversation, come back to Sloan Outlaw."

Leslie glanced at her watch. "I want to take a nap before dinner."

"Okay. When do the two of you leave for Sloan's cabin?"

Carmen would have to remind her of that. "A week from today."

"You're going to enjoy yourself."

Leslie rolled her eyes. "How would you know?"

"Because Sloan is a nice guy."

"You've never met him, Carm."

"I saw a glimpse of him before he left that wedding reception. Besides, as far as I'm concerned, he proved just how nice he truly is by saving your company. And another thing, Les."

Leslie knew Carmen was on a roll, although she wished otherwise. "What?"

"There's something you tend to forget."

"And just what do I tend to forget?"

"That you hurt Sloan when you believed that woman's lies. He didn't hurt you, you hurt him. So the way I see it, he's entitled to be a little salty about it. I'll talk to you later."

Eight

Sloan knocked on Leslie's hotel room door, and when she opened it, he tried not to show any reaction. Doing so was difficult. Why did she have to look so darn good in that red velvet pantsuit? The blazer seemed tailor-made and flowed over her slacks precisely. And that color was perfect for this holiday season. He thought the dangling earrings complimented her hairstyle and gave her a sexy look.

Only when he was certain he had retained control of his senses did he say, "You look nice."

"Thanks. I just need to grab my coat."

Although she didn't invite him in, she left the door open, so he remained in the doorway and watched her grab her wool coat off the bed. The same bed she would be sleeping in tonight. He could envision her in that bed, sleeping on her side, which was her favorite position. It was a position he'd liked for her as well, especially whenever they slept spoon style with her backside resting smack against his groin.

"I'm ready, Sloan."

She'd come to stand in front of him while his thoughts had been a million miles away. Well, in truth, they had been only as far as the distance to that bed. After closing the door behind her, they walked side by side, in sync, toward the elevator. "Where are we dining?" she asked him.

"I told you earlier, with the Yules."

She glanced over at him, and the moment their gazes met, he felt a stirring in the pit of his stomach. "I didn't mean with whom, but where?"

"We're dining in their home."

"Oh."

"Do you have a problem with that?"

"No."

"Like I told you, they're an older couple, and I understand Mrs. Yule loves to cook and wanted to prepare a meal for us."

"That was nice of her," Leslie said as they stepped into the elevator.

They said nothing during the short ride down to the first floor. Just as well, Sloan thought.

"I got a call from my attorney around an hour ago," she said as they stepped outside.

He glanced over at her as he held the door. Their four hours of daylight had ended hours ago, and it was dark outside. At least for the time being, it had stopped snowing. "And?"

"And he said the paperwork your attorney sent to him looks good. It included everything you said it would."

"Did you think it wouldn't, Leslie? I only wanted to help you, not take your company from you."

"I know that, Sloan. I wish you wouldn't dissect everything I say and make it an issue of trust."

When they reached the car, he opened the door for her and said, "If I am making it one, maybe you need to ask yourself why."

"And maybe you need to act like you accepted my apology like you claimed you did."

Sloan didn't say anything. Instead he waited for her to get in and snap her seat belt in place before closing the car door.

"Welcome to our home."

"Thank you." Leslie could not help staring at the white-bearded, hefty man who opened the door wearing a pair of overalls. Her eyes widened, immediately thinking that he looked just like…

"I know what you're thinking," Rudolph Yule said with a huge grin on his face. "The reason I look so much like Santa Claus is deliberate. This time of year, I pretend I'm the jolly ole guy himself here at North Pole. So did my father, grandfather and great-grandfather. And one day I figure my oldest son will do it as well. I guess you can say it's been a tradition in the Yule family for generations."

"Who was Santa here twenty-three years ago?" Sloan

asked. He stood beside her, and when he accidentally brushed against her, a tremble ran through her body.

"That was Dad. He passed away twelve years ago."

"I'm sorry to hear of his passing. I took a picture with him as Santa at that gift shop in town when I was ten. I still have the picture we took together," Sloan said.

Rudolph Yule gave a hearty laugh, one Leslie thought actually made his belly shake. "Probably you and a million other kids. You wouldn't believe the number of adults who took photos with Dad or Granddad and now bring their kids back for photos. Both Dad and Granddad left big shoes for me to fill. Come to the living room and sit by the fire. My wife is happy you're here for dinner."

"We're happy to be here," Sloan said, placing his hand at the center of Leslie's back. Her heart skipped, and when she glanced over at him, she knew he'd felt something, too. Yet he didn't remove his hand.

The huge room had what Leslie thought was the largest fireplace she'd ever seen. It made the entire area feel warm and inviting. What really caught her attention was the massive, beautifully decorated Christmas tree that sat on one side of the room. It had to be over fourteen feet tall, with thousands of twinkling lights.

"That tree is gorgeous," Leslie said.

"One hundred school children from all over Alaska get to come here on a field trip the week before Thanksgiving to help me decorate Santa's Christmas tree," an elderly woman said, coming into the room.

The older woman gave both Leslie and Sloan hugs, showing she was just as friendly as her husband. Leslie thought she looked just like anyone would envision Mrs. Claus to look…if there had been a real one. She was wearing a red dress with a white apron, and her round face and high cheekbones seemed to make her gray hair glow.

"I hope the two of you are hungry," Mrs. Yule said.

"We are," Sloan replied. "Something smells good."

"It's my moose stew."

"I love moose stew," Leslie said as they followed the Yules into the dining room. "My mother used to make it all the time."

There was a long table that seated at least twenty people. That prompted her to ask, "You have a large family?"

The older woman smiled. "Yes, we do. Rudy and I have ten children and six grands. They all work in the toy factory and are looking forward to meeting the two of you tomorrow when you're given a tour of the factory."

Leslie smiled. "I look forward to meeting them."

Always the gentleman, Sloan pulled out the chair for her before taking his own. Dinner was served immediately, and the food was delicious. Mrs. Yule had baked yeast rolls that were so good they practically melted in Leslie's mouth. Even the wine, which had been produced in a neighboring town, was delicious. The after-dinner dessert was a Christmas cake.

Because this was a business dinner meeting, the Yules sat down and thanked Sloan profusely for coming to their rescue and saving their company. A company he had yet to see. They admitted they hadn't known about the hostile takeover attempt by Martin Longshire until it was too late to do anything about it.

That made Leslie say, "I understand he went after your company for personal reasons."

Mrs. Yule glanced over at her and nodded. "That's true. He did it to get back at Merry."

"Mary?" Sloan asked.

"Yes, Merry, and that's M-e-r-r-y, and not M-a-r-y. She's our oldest daughter and the only member of the family who doesn't work in the family business. She always wanted to develop her skill as an artist, and years ago she got the chance to attend an art school in Paris. While living over there, she met Martin Longshire. He was living there as well, running his parents' business."

Mr. Yule then took up the story. "He saw Merry at some party and wanted her, although at the time she'd met Paul and the two of them were serious. It's my understanding that he even tried breaking them up, but he failed. Merry eventually married Paul. They still live in Paris and have three beautiful adult children."

"And you think that's the reason he wanted to take your company?" Leslie asked.

"Oh, we know that's the reason. After the takeover had gone through, he contacted Merry and told her what he'd done and why. He would have tried destroying Paul's company but couldn't. Paul's family is just as wealthy as Longshire. Paul would have helped us out but like we said earlier, we hadn't known about the hostile takeover attempt until it was too late to do anything about it."

The older woman then looked over at Sloan. "That's why we're glad you came along, Mr. Outlaw."

Sloan smiled. "I'm Sloan, remember." He then assured the older couple that he would work with them to improve their business and expand their market.

Leslie had never seen the business side of Sloan and had to admit that because of her mistrust, she'd been leery of his offer at first. But listening to him explain the ways he could help the Yules made her see him through the older couple's eyes. They saw his offer for what it was—a genuine desire to help someone in need. The Yules were gracious and had not questioned his motives the way she had. It was obvious they appreciated his help, especially after dealing with the likes of Martin Longshire.

It was fascinating to hear how the Yules and their family manufactured toys all year long, stockpiling the merchandise to have the items ready to ship out beginning the week before Thanksgiving. It seemed they had a good routine going, and she listened while Sloan made a number of suggestions. His vast knowledge of various business models and the way he was able to recommend several he felt would be ideal for them was amazing.

While Mr. Yule showed Sloan his train set collection, Leslie offered to help Mrs. Yule clear the table. The kitchen was just as massive as the other room, but Leslie figured when so many kids once lived there, you would need a lot of cooking space.

"I think you and Mr. Outlaw make a stunning couple. The two of you will have beautiful babies."

Leslie nearly missed her step. She then quickly corrected the woman. "Oh, it's not like that. Sloan and I aren't a couple."

The woman only smiled and said, "If not, then you should be. Do you know what I see when I see the two of you?"

"No. What do you see?" she asked, curious to know.

Mrs. Yule smiled. "I see forever."

Forever? Leslie wasn't sure how the woman could see something like that, but she decided not to ask. Instead, she changed the subject by inquiring about some of the places to tour while in town. The first place Mrs. Yule suggested was Santa House, where there was a gift shop that sold their toys.

As Leslie continued to help the older woman clear the table and put things away, she couldn't help but think about what the woman had said about her and Sloan.

"So, what do you think of the Yules?" Sloan asked as they left the older couple's home.

"I like them. They certainly appreciate you saving their company from Longshire. And to know he went after their company for the same reason he went after mine—because years ago, a woman he wanted hadn't wanted him—is truly sad. How can one man be so despicable?"

"I have no idea. He definitely takes holding grudges to a whole other level, that's for sure." Sloan then glanced up into the sky. "It's a beautiful night, isn't it?"

She looked up as well. "Yes, it is. The sky is so

bright, and you can see the stars so clearly. It's like you can reach up and touch one."

"According to Mr. Yule, tonight will be the best time to see the Northern Lights in this area," he said.

"Is it really?"

Sloan smiled upon hearing the excitement in her voice. "Yes," he said, opening the car door for her. "Do you want to see them? Mr. Yule gave me directions to the best observation point in town." Most Alaskans knew Fairbanks and North Pole were the best places in the state to view the Northern Lights, since both towns were located inside the Auroral Oval.

She glanced at her watch. "What time will it appear?"

"A little after midnight?" That meant they would be sitting together in a parked car for an hour. That was something they hadn't done since their college days.

Leslie finally nodded and said, "We only get a glimpse of the lights in Wasilla, definitely not what you can see in this section of Alaska, and I really would like to see it from here. Besides, I'm sure a number of others will be parked at that observation point as well."

Did her latter comment mean she had a problem being parked alone with him? In that case, Sloan wouldn't mention that the location Mr. Yule had suggested was a very private one and there wouldn't be others around.

"I can't wait to see the place where the toys are manufactured tomorrow," he said, changing the subject.

"I can't, either. Thanks for inviting me along, Sloan."

A part of him wished she wouldn't thank him for

everything he did. But how would he feel if she didn't show her gratitude? He knew Leslie, and one of the reasons he had fallen in love with her was that she never took anyone's kindness lightly.

As they drove through the streets of North Pole, she commented on how it appeared every street had a Christmas theme. There was Mistletoe Road, Snowman Lane and Kris Kringle Drive, just to name a few.

When he thought things had gotten too quiet between them, at a traffic light, he glanced over at her and said, "There's a place I visited a few years back in the lower forty-eight called Christmas, Florida."

She lifted a brow. "Is that a real city?"

He chuckled. "Yes. It's small, but a city nonetheless. It's located not far from Orlando. There's this huge Christmas tree at the entrance to the town that's kept decorated all year round. Some of the residents even keep their homes lit with Christmas lights all year."

"I bet that can get expensive," she said.

Sloan glanced back at the road when the traffic light changed. It was good timing, too, since he hadn't been able to *not* look at her mouth and remember the number of times he'd kissed it. "I'm sure it can be, but I would hope the electric company gives them some kind of break for promoting the town's theme."

"I would hope so, too."

He made a turn off the only main road in town and headed into a more rural area. "I've never been somewhere so dark at night."

Sloan chuckled. "Missing streetlights already, are you?"

"Yes, I'm a city girl, so I'm used to them."

"And that's another reason why you don't get to see the Northern Lights as well as we can in this section. This is a rural area. Not much of that in Wasilla," he said.

"True." She leaned in to look out the windshield at the sky. "It's even more beautiful out here."

A few minutes later, he made the last turn Mr. Yule had instructed him to make. It was so dark, he had to hit his high beams to see in front of him. He then brought the car to a stop. "We are here."

She glanced around. "Where are the others?"

He glanced over at her. "What others?"

"You said this would be a good night to watch the Northern Lights and this was the best observation point."

"It is."

"I assumed other people would be parked here."

"No, there aren't any others. This is private land, and we're all alone."

Nine

They were all alone...

Leslie wondered why that thought bothered her when it shouldn't. They had been alone on the flight coming here, but that was different. They hadn't been in a parked car in the middle of nowhere in years. Total blackness surrounded them.

However, they did have a full moon in the sky that provided some light in the interior of the car. Out of the corner of her eye, she saw Sloan's head tilt back against the headrest. She sighed. Sharing a parked car on a secluded lot with Sloan Outlaw was not a good idea.

She was about to suggest they forget about seeing the Northern Lights when he asked, "Have you ever thought about expanding your business beyond Alaska, Leslie?"

Sloan's question made her realize whatever sexual

chemistry she felt was one-sided. The only thing on Sloan's mind right now was business. She should have been grateful for that, but she couldn't help feeling a little let down. There was a time when being in a parked car with him automatically meant only one thing. Was he letting her know those days were long gone?

"I haven't had time to think about it. Dad was contemplating it, though. He'd thought about testing the market by doing an exclusive line in Hollywood."

"Hollywood?"

"Yes. There are several makeup artists there who only use our brand. We ship it directly to them." After shifting in her seat, she said, "Why do you ask?"

"I was just wondering. Like I was telling the Yules over dinner, companies that are just doing business in Alaska are missing out on bigger markets."

Leslie nodded. "I'll eventually get there. After Dad died, my main concentration was holding on to the company. I got wind of what Martin Longshire was up to the day after Dad's funeral. Unlike what he did with the Yules, with me he wasn't keeping his plans a secret."

She then recalled that she'd never asked how Sloan had known Cassidy Cosmetics was under a hostile takeover. "How did you know what Longshire was up to with my company, Sloan?" He switched on the car's heater. She appreciated that and figured her occasional shivers had given her away.

"It was a conversation Redford shared with me at Tyler and Keosha's wedding. Evidently he slept with one of Longshire's employees, who shared the plan."

"I see."

When the car got quiet, she decided to keep conversation going and asked, "So what are your plans for Christmas?"

Sloan figured it would not be a good idea to tell her that his plan for Christmas was her. She knew he wanted her for Christmas. Now he couldn't dismiss that things went a lot deeper than that. Even after they spent a week together at the cabin, she would still be alone for the holidays.

For days he'd been battling with the thought that he didn't care, only to finally accept that he did. As absurd as it might sound, he wanted her to spend the holidays with him even after the time they spent at the cabin. It would be her first Christmas without her father, and he didn't want to think of her hurt and all alone.

Why he even gave a damn he wasn't sure, but he did.

Knowing she was waiting for his response, he said, "I told you about my cousins, the Westmorelands."

"Yes."

"Since getting to know them, it has become a habit to spend the holidays with them."

She lifted a brow. "Why?"

He wasn't surprised she asked, because she knew how, thanks to Bart, their family used to be considered unsociable and unfriendly years ago. "We have a lot in common and enjoy spending time with them. Besides, their charitable foundation holds this huge event every year around the holidays. It's a meaningful time together, and it's also fun. We consider it family bonding time." He hoped she would get to see firsthand how meaningful things were for the Westmoreland family, a family the Outlaws were now a part of.

All of a sudden, he heard her sharp intake of breath. He followed her gaze and saw what had caught her attention. The Northern Lights. Prisms of color flooded the skies in a brilliant display. He thought now what he thought every time he saw it—it was a powerful thing. While growing up, he'd always felt fortunate that the state where he was born could claim this beauty in a way others could not.

"I have to get out of the car," Leslie said, opening the car door.

Following her lead, Sloan got out as well. Outside, it seemed as if the sky was right there on top of them. Mr. Yule had been right. Sloan had seen the Northern Lights from several sites over the years, but he thought this particular location was the best.

He and Leslie were standing side by side in front of the car. When he felt her shiver, he turned to see her tighten her coat and scarf around herself while still looking up into the sky. "Beautiful."

Sloan had to agree. However, he was not looking up at the sky but at her. She was as beautiful as the Northern Lights. In fact, the sky's prism seemed to highlight her features in a way that brought out her beauty even more.

"Yes, it is beautiful," he said and looked up into the sky. The last thing he wanted was to give away what he was thinking.

He then decided to tack on, "Mr. Yule was right. This is the best place to see it." When she shivered again, he instinctively wrapped his arms around her to share his heat. Wordlessly, they stood together, looking up at the sky.

Sloan wasn't sure how long they stood there, but the temperature had dropped even more, and they needed to get back inside the car. He was about to tell her that when he saw her staring at him.

At that moment, something happened that he hadn't expected. He momentarily forgot that she was the reason for his first heartbreak. That she was the reason he refused to fall in love again. Instead, he was remembering other times when they had gone to a secluded area, gotten out of the car and stood beneath an Alaskan sky. Usually, they would kiss.

They had never shared a kiss under the Northern Lights. Why did he want to do so now? He mentally told himself to release her and step back, suggest they get in the car and leave. However, for some reason he couldn't do that. Instead, he gave in to temptation and leaned in to capture her mouth with his.

The moment their mouths touched, the taste he'd thought he had forgotten renewed itself in every part of his being.

Ten years ago, he and Leslie had been a lot younger, carefree and in love. Now they were older, serious-minded and no longer in love. But that didn't stop his gloved hands from moving over her shoulders while his mouth feasted on hers. And when his hands lowered to her back, he could feel her heat even through his gloves and her coat.

She was kissing him back. That let him know she

was enjoying the reunion of their mouths as much as he was. When his tongue took hold of hers, he tried to convince himself he wasn't retaking a claim. He was merely enjoying the moment. Relishing her taste. However, a part of him knew he was doing more when he began sucking on her tongue with a hunger he felt right in his groin. Wrapping his arms around her tightly, he nearly groaned when even with the thickness of their coats, he could feel his solid, hard erection pressed between her thighs.

There was no telling how long they would have stood there kissing in the freezing cold beneath the Northern Lights if they hadn't heard the sound of a moose call. One that was too close for comfort.

Breaking off the kiss and releasing her, he said, "I think we better get back in the car, Leslie."

When she released a long sigh and then nodded, he escorted her back to her side of the car and opened the door for her. "Thanks."

"You're welcome," he said.

After getting back inside, he started the engine to warm up the car. He also wanted to warm her up. Thoughts of pulling her across the seat and into his lap to kiss her again, while his hands opened her coat to touch her everywhere, filled his mind.

She squashed that idea when she said, "I'm ready to go back to the hotel now, Sloan."

He wasn't surprised that she regretted their kiss and was ready to bring this night to an end. Obviously that kiss had shaken her up as much as it had him.

"All right."

"And, Sloan?"

He glanced over at her. He figured this was when she would tell him their kiss had been a mistake. "Yes, Leslie?"

"Thanks for sharing the Northern Lights with me," she said in an almost whisper. "I enjoyed it."

A part of him was tempted to ask if she'd enjoyed sharing a kiss with him as well, but he thought better of doing so. "Don't mention it."

While putting the car in gear to leave the observation point, he knew he would be carrying the memory of the kiss they'd shared under the Northern Lights around with him for a while.

Ten

Was Sloan staring at her more than usual? Specifically, her mouth? Leslie couldn't help pondering that question when they'd arrived at the Yuletide Toy Factory the next morning. He had just opened the car door for her, and now his gaze seemed to be glued to her lips.

The same thing had happened earlier over the breakfast they'd shared at the hotel. More than once she had looked up from her meal to find him staring at her. Namely, her mouth. Had he been reminded of the kiss they'd shared last night?

It had been a kiss she hadn't expected, but she wasn't surprised she'd gotten wrapped up in it like she had. Sloan had been a great kisser, and it was obvious nothing had changed. If anything, he was better at it.

He was older, more experienced, and the lips that

had taken her mouth last night had contained a fire she hadn't known back then. The intensity of the way their mouths mated was the reason she hadn't been able to settle into a peaceful sleep when they'd returned to the hotel. Instead, she had lain awake most of the night reliving it.

As she walked beside Sloan, she wondered if he'd had a hard time sleeping like she had. Probably not. She was certain he had kissed a lot of women since her. That made her wonder how she compared.

She also wondered about something else. Had their kiss reminded him of how things had once been for them? Did he now regret kissing her? If that was the case, then he could only get mad at himself, because he had initiated it. Not her. But she'd gone along with it. Honestly, what had he expected? She'd always been putty in his arms, especially when it came to his kisses.

However, his touch was another weakness of hers, she thought, when he touched her arm to escort her to the door of the building. "This place is huge," she said when they reached the entrance. Before she could stop herself, she took a quick look over at him. He looked handsome this morning. But then, Sloan always looked handsome.

"Yes, it is."

Sloan knocked, and immediately the door swung open and a jolly-looking Mr. Yule stood there with a huge grin on his face. "Welcome to Santa's workshop," he said, moving aside to let them in. The moment she walked over the threshold, Leslie took it all in. Although there were no elves, just regular people busy stocking boxes, it still reminded her of what Santa's workshop should look like. It might have something to do with the fact that everyone was wearing red Christmas hats with white cuffs. There was another decorated Christmas tree and a group of life-size reindeer that seemed to be looking on the process with their approval.

"This is the packaging area. Next, I want to show you where everything is manufactured," Mr. Yule said excitedly. "All our toys are made of wood," he told them.

She raised a brow. "No plastic?"

"Not a bit," Mr. Yule said, opening a huge door. They followed him in. "Wood lasts longer and is more durable," the older man said. "However, because wood is heavier in weight, that has always been a major problem for us when it comes to shipping costs."

"Not anymore," Sloan said, scanning the area where the toys were being manufactured.

Leslie looked over at him. "Why will it no longer be a problem?" she asked.

Sloan glanced at her. "Since my family owns a transport company, the cost of shipping will no longer be a major issue."

She nodded. "I see." In a way she saw more than Sloan probably wanted her to. Just like she'd suspected, he was setting up the company for success and making sure they would be able to hold their own if Longshire ever got the mind to come after them again.

Mr. Yule looked at his watch. "I need to leave to get on my post as Santa at the Santa House. Make sure you two stop by to visit me there. My oldest son, Garland, will continue on with the tour."

Leslie lifted a brow. "Garland?"

Mr. Yule laughed. "Yes, Garland. I also have sons named Cane, Kris, Nicholas and Sleigh. We told you about our daughter Merry last night. There's also Holly, Star, Noel and Angel."

Garland, a man in his fifties, who was smaller in stature than his father and whose beard wasn't as massive and white, led them through the rest of the building. They watched toys being made and then, in another section, watched as toys were hand-painted.

At the end of the tour, Mrs. Yule prepared lunch. That's when Leslie and Sloan got to meet the other adult Yule children and grandchildren, who all worked at the factory and who all had names connected with Christmas. They were appreciative of Sloan saving the family business.

When she and Sloan were back in the car after leaving the toy factory, he asked, "So what do you think?"

She glanced over at him. "I think it's a tidy operation, and although most of the employees are related, they seem to work well together."

"I noticed that as well and think of it as a positive," Sloan said. "It's obvious they take pride in the products their family produces."

She thought so as well. When neither seemed to have anything else to add, she thought it would be a good time to bring up a subject she knew they'd been avoiding—their kiss. Although she didn't regret it, she knew it was something they should not do again. "I think we need to talk about that kiss, Sloan."

"What about it?"

"It shouldn't happen again."

He released a smooth chuckle. "It will happen again, Leslie. However, if it will make you feel better, I will let you initiate it next time."

"Then I don't have to worry about it happening again."

"Okay."

Okay? "What is that supposed to mean?"

"Okay means I don't agree or disagree. Whatever happens will happen."

When he pulled into the parking lot of Santa House, he switched off the car and said, "We're leaving early in the morning."

She lifted a brow. "I thought our flight didn't take off until noon."

"It doesn't. I need to do a pit stop in Fairbanks for some papers."

Leslie nodded. "At your office?"

"No, at my home." He turned in his seat to face her. "Do you have a problem with that?"

"Should I have a problem with it?"

He shrugged. "I don't see why you should when we'll only be there for a few minutes."

There was no need to tell him that a lot could happen behind closed doors in a few minutes. As if he'd read her thoughts, he said, "This time next week, we'll be spending a week together in seclusion at the cabin on Kodiak Island. I hope you're not nervous about being alone with me."

She rolled her eyes. "I am alone with you now, Sloan.

I was also alone with you on the flight here and will be alone with you on the flight back."

Sloan smiled. All kinds of sensations flooded her stomach. Drawing in a quick breath, she broke eye contact with him and turned to unlock her door.

"I've got that," he said, opening his own car door to sprint around the front of the car to open the door for her.

"Thanks."

"You are welcome," he said, taking her hand to help her out.

The moment their hands touched, she felt heat, even though they were wearing gloves. It had snowed heavily last night and was snowing now with temperatures below zero. Regardless of the fact that it was cold as the dickens on the outside, some kind of fire was consuming her on the inside. It didn't take a rocket scientist to know she was in trouble with Sloan.

She may have bitten off more than she could chew.

Sloan glanced around Santa House. It seemed a lot larger than he remembered as a child, and when he asked their tour guide about it, the young lady said that over the years, due to remodeling, it had nearly doubled in size.

He noticed a lot of parents and their kids were headed to where he knew Mr. Yule was holding court as Santa. Leslie headed to the gift shop, and he instinctively followed her.

"I want to buy one of those wooden train sets for Elan."

He lifted a brow. "Who is Elan?"

"Carmen's nine-year-old nephew."

That told him nothing, since he had no idea who Carmen was, either. Evidently seeing the bemused look on his face, she added, "Carmen was my roommate at Howard, and someone I consider my best friend. She was my plus-one at Tyler and Keosha's wedding."

He nodded. "She lives in Alaska?"

"Heavens, no. She hates cold weather, but I managed to talk her into spending Thanksgiving with me. No easy feat, I assure you. Even with the weather, we got to spend ten fun days together while she was here." Leslie smiled. "She claims she hasn't thawed out yet."

There had always been something about Leslie's smile, and he was convinced that smile was what had captured his interest from the first. "And she has a nine-year-old nephew?"

"Yes. He's her sister's son. I think he will love the train."

When they reached the shelves, he saw there were only two left, and he quickly pulled one off the shelf for Leslie. "Got it."

"Thanks," she said as they headed for the checkout counter. "I think it's great that they'll ship it for me, too." It didn't take long for her to pay for the item and complete shipping papers.

"Now," he said, taking her hand, "let's go see Santa. I am dying to know if you've been good this year."

She threw back her head and laughed. "You, who once admitted to always getting into trouble as a child and whose last name is Outlaw, are curious as to whether *I've* been good this year?"

He couldn't help laughing as well. "I guess that does sound rather amusing."

"Yes, it does."

While standing in line waiting their turn for Santa, a curious little girl standing in front of them, who looked to be about five years old, asked, "Where is your little boy or girl?"

Leslie smiled down at her. "We don't have one. I'm here to see Santa for myself."

"Oh. You've been bad?" the little girl asked, and Sloan thought the expression on her face showed she was trying to figure out what bad deed an adult could do to sit on Santa's lap and ask for forgiveness to get a toy.

"No, I haven't been bad," Leslie said, and Sloan had to cough to smother a laugh.

The little girl was about to ask Leslie another question when the child's mother gave Leslie an apologetic smile and shushed her daughter. "Kids still like you, I see," Sloan whispered.

"And I still like them," she said.

He didn't say anything as he recalled the number of times he'd thought about them sharing those children. Had things worked out the way he'd wanted them to, the way he'd assumed they would, she would have been the mother of his babies by now.

He quickly pushed that thought from his mind. It was a dream that had been destroyed and would never be resurrected.

That night before going to bed, he called Leslie to

tell her he had changed his mind about making a stop at his home in Fairbanks. What he hadn't told her was that while spending time with her today, he had experienced emotions he didn't want to feel. Emotions she seemed to elicit from him effortlessly.

The best thing to do was return Leslie to Wasilla. He needed to prepare mentally for their week together on Kodiak Island. Besides, there were a few behind-the-scenes things he needed to take care of regarding both her company and the Yuletide Toy Factory.

And there was Martin Longshire.

Already Sloan had gotten a call from Cole letting him know Longshire was digging into Sloan's affairs. Because he'd contacted Cole when he had, safeguards against tampering had been put in place. However, Sloan intended to track every move Longshire made. He would remain in Wasilla and work out of his hotel room instead of returning to Fairbanks. It really didn't make sense to go back and forth when he would need to return to Wasilla at the end of the week for Leslie.

He was determined not to have any contact whatsoever with Leslie this coming week. Putting distance between them for a few days would definitely help him get his head together where she was concerned. The strong attraction he'd felt toward her was something he could deal with as long as he kept things in perspective.

The one thing he refused to do was let Leslie Cassidy tangle with his mind ever again.

Leslie glanced over at Sloan when he parked the car at the airport. Since leaving the hotel, he'd said very few words to her. It was, she decided, a definite change compared to yesterday, when he'd been in a more talkative mood. Actually, she had picked up on his change of moods yesterday evening when he'd brought her back to the hotel.

"Thanks," she said after he opened the car door for her. Already he was moving away, toward the office where flight papers had to be filed.

Last night, he hadn't invited her to join him for dinner, which was just as well. She had ordered room service while watching a holiday movie on television. Afterward, she had showered and gotten in bed. That's when Sloan had called to tell her he wouldn't be stopping at his home in Fairbanks after all. She hadn't asked why he'd changed his mind, and he obviously hadn't felt the need to tell her.

It didn't take long for him to complete the necessary paperwork for them to take off. Unlike their earlier flight, when they'd engaged in a steady stream of conversation in the cockpit, the silence between them lasted through the entire flight.

More than once she found herself staring over at him while he maneuvered the plane through the less-than-friendly skies. It was snowing harder now than when they had arrived in North Pole, and she could tell Sloan's concentration was on piloting the plane through the rough weather.

When the plane took an unexpected dip, she drew in a sharp breath. He obviously heard it, and that's when he glanced over at her to ask, "You're okay, Leslie?"

She nodded, trying not to remember that's what he

would ask her after they'd made love. It had always been important to him to know that the intensity of their lovemaking had been all right with her and that she had enjoyed it as much as he had. "Yes, Sloan, I'm okay."

He resumed looking ahead, and she continued watching him, unable to look away. At that moment she felt a deep loss, a sense of extreme regret. It wasn't the first time she'd felt this way since discovering the truth, but it was hitting her harder today than ever before.

Why? Could it be the time she'd spent with Sloan over the past several days had made her realize just what she'd lost? Then there was the kiss they'd shared. She drew in a deep breath, definitely feeling the impact of knowing a man who'd once loved her as deeply as she'd loved him was lost to her forever.

Refusing to look over at him any longer, she thought about the plans for next week, when she would spend time with him at the cabin. Unlike the last time he'd asked her to spend a week with him, when she'd been all happy and excited about doing so, now she was dreading it.

Because he had invited her for one reason and one reason only: closure. Sleeping with her, if that's what happened, would be closure for him. He had loved her once. She knew Sloan. He had gotten over her like he'd said he had, but they needed a final chapter. There would not be a happy ending, just an ending.

Sloan had shared with her that closure was how he had dealt with his mother, too, after he'd discovered how much of a gold-digger Barbie was.

Bart hadn't had to take Barbie to court for custody of

Sloan. Instead, he'd given her enough money up front to keep her living in style for the rest of her life. Unfortunately, she hadn't known how to manage her finances. Sloan had heard from her a number of times over the years. Somehow, she had managed to reach out to him without Bart knowing about it. But she hadn't called because she was interested in Sloan's well-being. The only time she'd call was when she wanted him to hit Bart up for more money. When Sloan had refused, she cursed him out and told him she was glad he wasn't a part of her life.

Sloan had told Leslie how he had gone to see Barbie during his first year of college, after finding out where she was living. He had given her a check that had represented every last cent he'd had in his savings account— which had been close to fifty thousand dollars—and had told her he didn't want to see her ever again. Seeing his mother that day had been about closure.

Now Leslie figured she was just another closure he had to deal with. However, little did he know, but she needed closure as well. It was only when she got it that she could move on with her life.

Eleven

On Saturday morning Sloan arrived at Leslie's home just as he'd told her he would.

In the time since they had parted ways on Monday, he had thrown himself into his work, putting cautionary measures in place in case Longshire made a move in retaliation. He'd also met with members of his board to give them his take on the Yuletide Toy Factory and his recommendations for next year. He'd come up with a number of ideas, including one that would take the toy manufacturing company global.

Even with enough to keep him busy, he still had managed to think about Leslie. Not just a little, but a lot.

Tightening his coat around him, he rang her doorbell and remembered he'd stood in this same spot and at the same time last Saturday morning. How could a

Get up to 4
FREE FABULOUS BOOKS
You Love!

To thank you for being a loyal reader we'd like to send you up to 4 FREE BOOKS, absolutely free.

Just write "YES" on the Loyal Reader Voucher and we'll send you up to 4 Free Books and Free Mystery Gifts, altogether worth over $20, as a way of saying thank you for being a loyal reader.

Try **Harlequin® Desire** books featuring the worlds of the American elite with juicy plot twists, delicious sensuality and intriguing scandal.

Try **Harlequin Presents®** Larger-print books featuring the glamourous lives of royals and billionaires in a world of exotic locations, where passion knows no bounds.

Or **TRY BOTH!**

We are so glad you love the books as much as we do and can't wait to send you great new books.

So don't miss out, return your Loyal Reader Voucher Today!

Pam Powers

LOYAL READER
FREE BOOKS VOUCHER

woman he hadn't had any dealings with for ten years become a regular feature of his life now? Luckily for him, she was temporary. After their week together, she would go back to being out of sight and out of mind.

The door opened. "Good morning, Sloan."

Before he could respond, Leslie stepped out, and he instinctively moved back. "You're ready?" he asked, watching her lock her door.

"Yes." Then she headed toward the car, with a duffel bag on her shoulder and pulling a piece of luggage behind her.

He quickly followed her and then opened the trunk to place her luggage next to his before opening the car door for her. "Thanks."

"You're welcome," he said, closing the door.

Sloan slowed his pace as he walked behind the car to the other side, trying to pull himself together. He'd thought he had everything under control, and basically, he had—until she'd opened that door. Seeing her had done something to him, but he wasn't sure what. All he knew was that his heart had begun beating rapidly in his chest. It still was.

Opening the door, he slid behind the wheel and glanced over at her. She looked good. She smelled good. "You have everything?"

"Yes."

She was staring straight ahead, refusing to look at him. However, he couldn't stop looking at her. What was there about her this morning that had claimed his attention? That had desire flowing through his veins?

Like before, in deference to the cold weather, she was

covered from head to toe. Wool coat, gloves, boots and
a furry hat on her head. So what was there?

While he sat struggling with the dilemma, she
glanced over at him. "Is something wrong?"

The only thing wrong with him was that he had
missed her.

"Sloan?"

"No, nothing is wrong. I was just thinking about
something."

"What?"

He broke eye contact with her to start the car. "Nothing."

Sloan backed out of her driveway. This coming week
might be more of a challenge than he'd figured it would
be.

Leslie watched Sloan as he drove.

They would be spending an entire week together, and
if for one minute he thought he was going to ignore her
like he'd done on the trip home from North Pole, then
he was mistaken.

"I'd like a tree, please. A small one will work," she
said when he brought the car to a stop at a traffic light.

He glanced over at her. "What kind of tree are you
talking about?"

She smiled and didn't care that he didn't smile back.
"A Christmas tree, of course. I can't imagine spending
a week in a place not decorated for Christmas."

"I thought you said you wouldn't be celebrating it
this year," he said, breaking eye contact with her and
moving the car forward.

She shook her head. "I didn't say that. I told you this would be the first one without my father and I hadn't made any plans. I believe that Dad would want me to still enjoy the holidays, so I intend to do just that. Does this cabin have internet?"

"Yes, it has internet. We have our own tower, since this section of the island is pretty secluded. Walker's place, Hemlock Row, is about twenty miles away, so we share it with him."

"Walker Rafferty?"

"Yes. You remember Walker?"

She doubted any woman could forget the former Hollywood actor. When she'd accompanied Sloan home for Christmas that time, she had met Walker briefly. "Yes. How is he?" She remembered his wife and son had been killed in a car accident, which was the reason he had left Hollywood and returned to Alaska.

"Walker is fine. He remarried and has a set of twins."

"That's wonderful. Who did he marry?"

"Bailey. She's one of my Westmoreland cousins from Denver."

Leslie settled in her seat, listening to him tell her how the two had met and the beautiful family they had now. She thought it was a wonderful love story, one she knew she would never experience. It had been a long time since the thought of that bothered her, but it was bothering her now.

"This place is awesome, Sloan," Leslie said, entering the cabin and turning around in the huge living room. "It's definitely a lot larger than what I imagined."

Sloan entered after bringing in their luggage. She had removed her coat to reveal a pair of jeans and a chocolate-brown pullover sweater that clearly defined her curvy body. "Ready for a tour?" he asked.

"Yes."

He took her around the huge five-bedroom, four-bathroom cabin that was located deep in the mountains and backed up against the Shelikof Strait, a beautiful waterway that stretched from the southwestern coast of Alaska to the east of Kodiak Island.

Each bedroom had a huge stone fireplace, and the cabin had been built in such a way that the waterway could be seen from every bedroom. There was a huge kitchen, dining room and a massive family room.

Sloan figured what had impressed Leslie more than anything was the movable wall that led to an underground tunnel. Like he'd told her, he wasn't sure why his grandfather had built the secret passageway or why there was a gun case that held probably every type of weapon ever manufactured.

He went on to tell her that he and his siblings had their ideas. The repeating of those suspicions had pissed off their father so much he had ordered that they get rid of all the artillery. Unknown to him, they hadn't.

Sloan glanced at his watch. "Before we start losing daylight, I want to bring in more wood for the fireplace."

She nodded. "Do you need any help?"

"No, I got this."

It took him a few trips to fill the wood box inside before he got a sniff of something cooking. They hadn't talked about what they would be eating, although he'd told her about calling days ahead to make sure the refrigerator and freezer were fully stocked before they arrived. Sloan knew how much Leslie liked cooking and just how good she was at it.

"Something smells good," he said, coming into the house with a load of wood in his arms.

"I checked out the refrigerator and cabinets and saw there was everything I needed to make a pot of chili, a salad and some yeast rolls. I was listening to the weather report and heard it's supposed to start snowing tonight."

"That wouldn't surprise me." Kodiak Island was known not only for its bears but also for harsh weather.

"I took the bedroom across from yours, Sloan."

He glanced over at her, figuring that was her way of letting him know they wouldn't be sharing a bed tonight. "That's fine, Leslie. You can sleep in any bedroom you like."

"They're all beautiful."

Sloan chuckled. "I'm surprised you think that, since they were all decorated for the men in the family. All except Dad, since he hasn't been here in years."

"What about Charm?" she asked.

"Charm rarely comes here. She finds the place too secluded to suit her. The farthest she'll go whenever she visits Kodiak Island is Walker's ranch. She visits them often enough. She and Bailey forged a close relationship, and Charm has fallen in love with Walker and Bailey's twins. Charm hasn't been around a lot of babies before."

He glanced out the window. Unlike Fairbanks, which

usually only got four hours of daylight, Kodiak got six to seven hours. Now they had gone, and it was dark. "It's snowing already and coming down pretty hard," he said.

"Do you think we'll lose power?" she asked.

"There is always that possibility, but we have a fully operational generator. We're good."

What he'd told her was true, they were good, and before he left here, he intended to show her just how good together they could be.

"You've gotten quiet on me, Leslie."

She glanced across the dinner table at Sloan. Funny he should say that. When he had picked her up from her house, he'd barely said anything to her. But she'd been determined not to let him ruin what she'd decided would be a good time at the cabin, even if she had to entertain herself. Ignoring his brooding attitude, she had kept up a steady stream of conversation, even when his responses had been a nonchalant grunt.

His less-than-friendly attitude had begun thawing out when they had landed on Kodiak Island. Once settled in the rental car, he had told her about the time the cabin had become a stronghold against domestic terrorists, who'd been determined to kidnap his cousin Bane's wife. And while driving, Sloan had taken what he'd referred to as the scenic route that showed the beauty of the island with its abundance of hemlock trees. That had been the extent of what he'd said since picking her up.

And now he wanted to keep the conversation going?

"I've talked enough for today, Sloan. Didn't want

to wear out my welcome, since you've been in a less-than-friendly mood."

He nodded, as if he accepted her accusation. "I apologize for that. I had a lot on my mind this week businesswise, which is why you hadn't heard from me."

It hadn't bothered her when she hadn't heard from him. In a way, she was glad she hadn't. She'd needed time to unwind her brain and put everything in perspective. So whether he knew it or not, he'd done her a favor. "Did you get a lot accomplished?"

"Yes. I wanted a plan that could help the Yules. They run a tidy operation, but I've come up with other ways to make it grow."

She nodded. "I'm sure they will appreciate that. I like them. They are nice people."

"Yes, they are."

When he got up from the table and walked over to the counter to refill his coffee cup, she couldn't help but notice how good he looked in his jeans. When he'd been kneeling in front of the fireplace, she'd appreciated the way those same jeans stretched tight over his muscular thighs. Thighs that she remembered well. They would ride her hard while making love to her.

She'd always thought he looked good in pullover sweaters, since they captured the broadness of his chest so well. A chest she'd licked a number of times from top to bottom. He definitely looked good in the one he was wearing now. The tan color enhanced the darkness of his eyes. There was a lot about him that had changed physically. He was more built, and hard muscled, and solid, and—

"Would you like a refill on your coffee, Leslie?"

He had glanced over his shoulder to look at her. More than likely he had caught her staring. "No, thanks, I'm fine."

He smiled. "Yes, Leslie, you most definitely are."

She wished Sloan didn't have the ability to seduce her with just words alone.

"So what do you plan to do the rest of the day?" Sloan asked, coming to sit back down at the table.

"Read. I brought my e-reader, and it contains a number of books that I haven't started yet. And I am hoping we can get a tree tomorrow."

He nodded. "That shouldn't be a problem if the snow lets up. There are quite a few Fraser firs on this property."

She couldn't help but smile at that. "Then we need to go out early."

"And we will, granted it's not snowing." He took a sip of his coffee and then looked over at her in a way that made sensuous shivers race up her spine. "There's something I need to ask you, Leslie. Information that will be vital when we make love."

When we make love? Leslie wondered what part of *I will not sleep with you this week* he did not understand. He'd said he wanted her for Christmas, in his bed. She had explained to him, quite clearly, she'd thought, that the only thing he would get from her this week was companionship. "Need I repeat myself, Sloan? I will not be sleeping with you."

He smiled in a way that made more shivers race up her spine. "Then humor me and let me ask my question anyway."

Feeling frustrated, yet at the same time curious as to what he wanted to know, she asked, "What's your question?"

"When was the last time you made love with a guy?"

There was no way she would tell him that the last time had been with him. "Why do you want to know such a thing?"

She wondered if the kiss they'd shared had given her away. Could he tell that she kissed the same way she had ten years ago?

"Leslie?"

Instead of answering, she stood. "Even if I had agreed to sleep with you this week Sloan, the answer to your question would be that it's not any of your business. I'm not asking you about the last time you made love to a woman."

"You can if it interests you."

"It doesn't." After loading her dishes in the dishwasher, she turned around and said, "I'll see you in the morning, Sloan."

She could feel the heat of his gaze on her back when she walked out of the kitchen.

Twelve

Sloan leaned against one of the tall hemlock trees as he watched Leslie walk around several Fraser firs looking for what she'd said was the ideal Christmas tree. When he had awakened that morning, a part of him had hoped she had canned the idea of a Christmas tree. It didn't take long to see that she hadn't. She'd been up, dressed and had even prepared breakfast by the time he'd walked into the kitchen.

The breakfast of pancakes, bacon and eggs had been delicious. However, he didn't want her to assume that he expected her to do all the cooking, so he'd told her they would be sharing cooking duties. She told him she didn't mind cooking since she enjoyed it so much, and since her father died, she had no one besides herself to cook for.

Now here they were, on a part of the property where Christmas trees grew. She had checked out at least five but hadn't made up her mind about which one she would take. He recalled her saying she would settle on a small tree, but none of the five were what he considered small.

Like usual, she was dressed for the cold weather, but that didn't stop him from imagining what all she had on underneath that wool coat, boots and fur hat. He would give just about anything to be able to peel all that clothing off her when they got back to the cabin.

Last night, after watching the sway of her hips when she'd made her exit from the kitchen, he hadn't heard a peep out of her the rest of the night.

He had remained up for hours, enjoying a glass of wine while watching cop shows on television. When he had retired to his room, he had seen a light on under her door, which let him know that although she'd been quiet, she was still awake. Since he hadn't heard the sound of the television in her room, he figured she was reading.

Glancing at his watch, he looked back at her now and said, "How much longer will it take you to make up your mind about a tree, Leslie?"

She glanced over at him and smiled. He hadn't expected that smile, and it warmed him to the core. "Too cold out here for you, Sloan?"

"You know better than that."

She of all people knew how much he enjoyed cold weather. The colder the better. However, leaning against this tree with his gaze trained on her, he remembered another time he'd taken her to a Christmas tree farm. It had been a Sunday, and few people had been about.

He'd come close to tempting her to engage in a quickie behind the branches.

Thinking of that day made him recall the first time they'd met. It had been an extremely cold day in Anchorage when he and Redford had been headed to class. Leslie had sprinted across the yard in her haste and had bumped into them. Literally. She would have lost her footing and toppled over if he hadn't reached out and grabbed her. That would have been that, and he and Redford would have continued on their way, if she hadn't taken off that furry hat she'd been wearing to smile, apologize for bumping into him and thank him.

The moment he had looked into her eyes, he was convinced he had fallen in love right then and there. After thanking him, she had rushed off before he could get any information from her, including a name. He had thought of her constantly. Her eyes and smile had invaded his dreams. Just when he was convinced that he would never see her again, he had.

Her face had been on a campus flyer advertising her organization was accepting donations to help buy toys for disadvantaged children. Not only had he made a donation, but to spend time with her, he had joined her group. At first, he'd figured his attraction to her was merely sexual. But the more time he spent with her and the more he had gotten to know her, he'd accepted it was more than that.

"Okay, Sloan. This is the one I want."

Her words pulled him from the past and back to the present. He wasn't surprised that the one she'd finally settled on was the one he'd liked the best. "Are you sure that's the one?"

She smiled brightly. "Yes, I'm sure."

He nodded and picked up the saw by his feet, not believing she would spend time decorating a tree just to have it up for one week. He then thought of something. "We don't have any ornaments here," he said.

"No problem. I brought my own."

Sloan shook his head. Honestly, he wasn't surprised.

Leslie stood back as Sloan erected the tree near the window in the cabin's living room. It was beautiful and just what she needed to brighten her mood. Yesterday after dinner, she had taken a shower and gotten into bed but hadn't gone to sleep. Instead, she had pulled up her e-reader. From the sound of the television in the family room, it had been easy to guess Sloan was still a fan of cop shows.

And she'd known when he had decided to call it a night and go to bed. Although he'd tried to be quiet, she had heard him walk down the hall to his bedroom. She had held her breath, hoping he wouldn't knock on her door. He hadn't.

When she'd awakened to find it wasn't snowing, she had wanted to hurry and dress and get a tree before snow began falling again. When Sloan still had not awakened, she decided to go downstairs and prepare breakfast, convinced the smell of bacon would do the trick. She knew how much he loved bison bacon. That had worked. He had walked into the kitchen, fully dressed but still with that sleepy-sexy look.

"Are you sure this is where you want it?"

She blinked, recalling other times, during their love-making, when he would tease her relentlessly. He would rub his erection all over her, between her legs. Then as he entered her, he would teasingly ask, *Are you sure this is where you want it?* By then she would be nearly out of her mind. She would push upward to hold him inside her tightly, to show him that she'd known just where she wanted it.

"Leslie?"

From the look on his face, he was waiting for her to answer. There was no indication he had made a connection between what he'd asked now and the other times when he'd asked that same thing. "Yes, that location will work. I like that it's sitting in front of the window."

He rolled his eyes. "Need I remind you that we're out in the middle of nowhere, miles from civilization? The only person who might notice blinking Christmas lights are the bears."

"Thanks for reminding me, Sloan."

He threw his head back and laughed even though she honestly didn't see anything funny. He had told her the property surrounding the cabin was bearproof. In addition to the electric fencing, bear sensors were installed that not only emitted scents that bears detested but also blared music that bothered their eardrums. Besides, most bears hibernated during winter.

"Now that the tree is where you want it, I'm going to sit back and relax with a beer," he said.

"You're not going to help me decorate?"

"Nope. You can do a better job at it than I could. So, knock yourself out while I observe."

Leslie wasn't sure how she felt about him sitting there drinking beer, watching her. Knowing Sloan's eyes would be on her was not a comforting thought. He could look at her in ways that would make her feel naked even while she was wearing clothes. "Not sure I like the idea of you just sitting there observing. Don't you have anything better to do?"

"Yes."

"Then do it."

A smile curved his lips, and she had a feeling there was an ulterior motive behind it when he said, "I can't."

Why now of all times was she intensely attracted to him? She'd almost forgotten how he could seduce her with his eyes. "And why not?" she asked.

"Because what I really want to do is you, Leslie."

When Sloan left the living room and headed for the kitchen to get his beer, he couldn't help but smile at Leslie's expression. He had told her the truth—he wanted to do her, but he would settle for just sitting there and drinking his beer while watching that body in action. He had popped the top off his beer bottle when his cell phone rang. He recognized the caller. Garth. Pulling his phone out of the back pocket of his jeans, he clicked on.

"Yes, Garth?"

"I take it you made it to the cabin."

"Yes, I'm here. Arrived yesterday."

"Did you stop by Hemlock Row to visit with Walker and Bailey before you got there?"

Sloan took a swig of his beer. "I didn't have time. I wanted to get here and get settled before dark."

"That was a good idea."

At that moment Sloan heard Leslie call out to him to bring her a beer as well. Without thinking, he answered her in a loud voice, "Sure thing."

"I take it you're not alone, Sloan."

Garth's comment made Sloan realize his mistake. But then, he was a grown-ass man who could invite anyone he wanted to join him here. "No, I'm not alone." And because he knew from past experience that Garth had a way of finding out anything he wanted to know, Sloan decided to save him the trouble. "I invited Leslie to join me."

"Leslie Cassidy?"

"Yes, Leslie Cassidy," Sloan said, like there would be any other Leslie he would invite here.

"Does that mean the two of you are—"

"No!" Sloan said in a firm tone, squashing the assumption his oldest brother was about to make. "Leslie and I are not getting back together. I know how much she enjoys Christmas, and with her father's death, she has no family left to spend the holidays with. I saw no reason not to ask her to join me at the cabin this week."

Sloan knew the silence on Garth's end meant his oldest brother was analyzing what he'd said. So that Garth's thoughts wouldn't be headed in the wrong direction, Sloan added, "I could never love Leslie again."

"So, the two of you are merely friends."

Sloan frowned. *Friends? Not hardly.* "In all honesty,

Garth, I can't rightly say I even consider her a friend. She is nothing more than my business partner. Not the first time I've invited a business partner to the cabin."

"Yes, but the others were business partners who were also relatives, like Cole, Quade and the other Westmorelands. No woman has spent time with you at the cabin before, Sloan."

"How would you know?"

"I just do. Are you denying it?"

It was times like this when he wished his brother didn't know him so well. "There is nothing between me and Leslie, Garth."

"If you say so."

"I do say so, and there's no reason I shouldn't," Sloan said, ready to end the call.

"I hope you know what you're doing."

"Trust me, Garth, I know exactly what I'm doing."

"I just hope whatever plan you've concocted doesn't backfire on you."

Sloan lifted a brow. "Meaning what?"

"That you fall in love with her all over again. I know how much you loved her before."

Yes, of all people, Garth would know. He'd been the one to pull Sloan out of the pain and misery when Leslie had left. "Trust me, it won't happen. There is no way I can or will love her again."

"Possibly, however, I think you have forgotten something."

Sloan frowned. "What?"

"You should have told Leslie that her friend had come on to you, Sloan. Had you told her, there's a good chance she would not have believed the lie that woman told her. As far as I'm concerned, you share the blame for what happened."

You share the blame...

A short while later, Sloan was thinking about the words Garth had spoken as he sat on the sofa, slowly drinking his beer while watching Leslie decorate the tree. She was deliberately ignoring him, but he didn't mind, because he definitely wasn't ignoring her. Far from it. He was sitting with his legs stretched out in front of him, and he couldn't take his eyes off her. He was tuned in to every movement she made as she decorated the tree.

She wasn't trying to draw his attention. In fact, he would bet money she would have preferred he was someplace else, instead of sitting there, with a front-row view of what she was doing. Especially when he wasn't saying anything but pretending to listen to the Christmas music playing on her cell phone while she went about her business hanging ornaments on the tree. Where in the world had all that stuff come from?

"You're frowning, Sloan. Don't you like how the tree is taking shape so far?"

He blinked upon realizing what she'd said. "The tree is looking good," he said, as if the tree and not her had been holding his attention all this time. "I was just wondering where all this stuff came from. You had all this stuff left over after decorating your own tree?"

"No."

"Then you went out and bought all this stuff." It

was a statement more than a question, since it was the most logical one.

"That's precisely what I did. And my suitcase was mostly filled with decorations."

"You didn't mention anything about having a tree until we were on our way to the airport yesterday. What made you think I would go along with it?"

"I saw no reason why you wouldn't."

Yes, he could see her thinking that way. In the past he'd been known to give in to anything she'd wanted. It wasn't that she'd asked for much, and most of the time she asked only to help others. But whenever she did ask, he would move heaven and earth to give her whatever she wanted. That was then. So why would she think it would be the same now?

"The least you can do is flip the switch since I'm all finished now," she said, breaking into his thoughts.

She was staring up at the tree with a huge smile on her face, as if she was pleased with what she'd done. His gaze shifted off her to the tree. It looked good. "I assume you'll be taking this tree down before we leave here," he said, standing to move toward the light switch on the wall.

"Of course, but I don't plan to take all this stuff back to Wasilla with me."

He stopped walking and glanced over his shoulder at her. "What do you intend to do with it?"

"Leave it here. If someone else in your family decides to spend time here around the holidays and wants to put up a Christmas tree, then they will have the decorations to do so. It's my donation."

He couldn't see that happening but decided to let her think whatever she wanted. He flipped the light switch and watched as an even wider smile spread across Leslie's face when the tree came to life.

The tree wasn't overly done. Every ornament she'd selected was in the right place, and the lights seemed to illuminate the tree in a way that made his breath catch. At that moment, he wished more than just the bears could see her handiwork. There was no way anyone who saw this tree wouldn't eagerly anticipate the approaching holidays.

"It's beautiful, isn't it, Sloan?"

He shifted his gaze from the tree to her. The blinking lights seemed to say, "Look at me." And he was looking. Ten years ago, he had loved her to distraction, had wanted to make her a permanent part of his life, and now...

"The one thing I didn't get is a timer."

He lifted a brow at her comment. "A timer?"

"Yes. That way I could program the tree to come on and go off at certain times. Now we'll have to do it manually."

He shrugged. "That's not a problem."

"Glad you feel that way. I'm assigning you that job since you didn't help decorate."

He was about to tell her that anything dealing with the tree was her job since it was her idea, but he didn't want to ruin it for her. "Do you want me to prepare dinner, or are you still keen on the idea of doing all the cooking this week?" They had eaten leftover chili for lunch, and he'd told her more than once just how good it had been. But then, breakfast had been good as well.

"I'd like to prepare dinner if you don't have a problem with me doing so. However, if you ever want to spend time in the kitchen with me or without me, please let me know," she said.

She didn't have to worry about that happening. Had he been here alone, Sloan would have been just fine getting by on easy meals he could prepare quickly. But he wasn't here alone, and Leslie loved to cook and had a way of turning an easy meal into a masterpiece.

A short while later, he was back to sitting in front of the Christmas tree, watching the blinking lights while his ears picked up the sound of Leslie moving around in the kitchen as she prepared dinner. He didn't want to think that if things hadn't ended between them ten years ago, this could very well be the same scenario... with them here spending Christmas at the cabin. He'd like to think they would have had at least two or three kids by now. Maybe she would have a position in Outlaw Freight Lines or he a position at Cassidy Cosmetics. Hell, there was no reason they would not have been able to manage both.

While dating, they had never talked about marriage. He'd just assumed it was a foregone conclusion and figured she'd thought so as well. Proposing to her at this cabin would have been a surprise to her, but it was something he'd wanted to do for a long time. He had seen forever in their future. Not only had he seen it, but he had wanted it with a yearning that went down to the very core of his existence.

Sloan drew in a deep breath, trying to regain control of his thoughts and accept that none of those plans happened. He'd never gotten the chance to propose, and there was no forever for them. A part of him wished he could forget about their past and handle her like he would handle any other business partner. Just like he'd told Garth, Leslie wasn't the first business partner he'd invited to the cabin.

But Garth had been right as well when he'd said it wasn't the same. Sloan and Leslie had history. Personal history. He didn't want to think of what Garth's reaction would be if he knew why she was spending a week here, and the stipulation Sloan had placed on her to save her company.

You share the blame...

He rubbed his hand down his face, feeling like an ass. He'd had hopes for how this week was supposed to pan out. Granted Leslie had said she wouldn't be sleeping with him, but he'd felt the attraction that was still there between them, and he was banking on her feeling it, too.

Garth was right. Sloan did share the blame for their breakup. Just like she should have trusted him, he should have made her aware of the situation when that trust might be challenged.

Standing, he began pacing, deep in thought. After a short while, he knew there was only one thing to do. Over dinner he would tell her to pack up her things tonight so he could fly her back to Wasilla in the morning. He would no longer hold her to the proposition that had been part of his plan to settle a score. A vengeance he'd refused to acknowledge until now.

But what about him not wanting her to spend the holidays alone?

At that moment he decided Leslie spending the holidays alone was better than her spending them here with him for all the wrong reasons.

Thirteen

Leslie glanced across the table at Sloan. She had cooked baked salmon with cabbage, rolls and slices of Yukon Gold potatoes. She'd even made a berry pie for dessert. Although he seemed to be enjoying the dinner she'd prepared, he wasn't saying much. Something was up and she could sense it, but she had no idea what that something was. She knew better than to try to figure out Sloan or his mood.

After decorating the tree, she felt good. The last thing she wanted was for Sloan to put a damper on her own mood. She definitely had no plan to ruin it by engaging in any type of verbal sparring with him. After dinner she would do what she'd done last night, what she intended to do every night, which was to go into her bedroom, shower and then curl up with her e-reader.

"I made a decision about something an hour ago, Leslie."

She looked up from buttering her bread and held his gaze. "A decision about what?"

"It was a decision about you. I will no longer hold you to the stipulation that you be here this week."

What exactly was he saying? "Meaning what, Sloan?"

"Meaning you need to pack tonight, because I'm taking you back to Wasilla in the morning. Nothing will change as far as my being your business partner, but I will now admit what I asked you to do here was unfair."

Yes, it had been, and she couldn't help wondering what had made him realize it. "Like I told you, Sloan, I wasn't going to sleep with you anyway."

"I had hoped to seduce you."

Leslie frowned at him. He sounded so confident, as if he believed he would have been successful in doing so. Back in the day, when she was his girlfriend, he'd never had to seduce her into anything, because she'd always been willing and ready to share his bed. That was then and this was now. And now he wanted her gone, so she would never know the extent of his seduction skills.

"I'll start packing tonight and will be ready to leave in the morning," she said, standing. After walking over to the sink to place her dishes in it, she then walked out of the kitchen.

Deciding to take a shower before packing, she began stripping off her clothes. She liked this cabin, and although leaving here was the last thing she honestly wanted to do, maybe it was for the best. Sloan obviously thought so.

In the privacy of the shower, while water cascaded down her naked body, she closed her eyes and remembered those times when she and Sloan would shower together. Recalling how he would touch her all over, fill her with an intensity of sexual longing and desire she hadn't felt in years.

Showering with him was something she'd always looked forward to doing. The last time it had been in a hotel room the night before he was to fly out to prepare the cabin for their upcoming spring break week. The reason she hadn't left when he had was because of an exam in one of her classes.

Because Redford and Tyler had been Sloan's roommates at his apartment, and Sarah had been hers, the only time they'd had any privacy was when Sloan reserved a hotel room for them. He'd done that a lot because he'd said he wanted them to spend as much private time together as possible.

Although her father had been disappointed in her decision to spend spring break with Sloan instead of coming home, he had understood. He'd known how much she loved Sloan, and after meeting Sloan, he was convinced Sloan loved her, too.

Getting out the shower, she dried off while thinking Sloan would never know how hard it had been to decorate that tree with his eyes on her the entire time. She had tried to ignore him, had refused to look over at him, but she had been conscious of him sitting there, his masculine scent and the vibes she'd felt emitting from him.

Had he felt the strong sexual chemistry between them, too? Was that why he'd decided to take her away?

Had he seen seducing her as a double-edged sword? Would he be tempting himself as well?

It truly didn't matter what had made him change his mind. He no longer wanted her here, and she didn't want to be here.

But, as she slipped into her nightgown, she knew that was a lie. She had begun looking forward to spending time here this week. She loved the cabin, she loved the tree, she loved being able to clear her mind of Cassidy Cosmetics business and do something she hadn't done in a while, which was read for pleasure.

She didn't want to think about returning home to spend the rest of the holidays alone. It was the new normal, and one she needed to get used to.

Leslie pulled her luggage from underneath the bed and then she heard the knock on her bedroom door. She wondered if Sloan had changed his mind and had decided not to wait until morning but to take her home tonight. "Just a minute."

Grabbing her bathrobe off the bed, she quickly put it on and tightened the belt around her waist before opening the door. Sloan stood there, frowning.

"What do you want, Sloan?"

"Forget about packing. There's no way I can take you home tomorrow."

She crossed her arms over her chest and frowned back at him. "And why not?"

"I just got a call from Walker. In case I hadn't been paying attention to the weather reports, he wanted to let me know about the severe snowstorm headed this way. It's the worst this area has seen in years."

* * *

Sloan figured Leslie wouldn't be happy about the forecast, but instead of disappointment in her expression, he saw concern.

"Is there anything we need to do tonight, Sloan? Are you sure the generator will work? Do you have any idea how long the snowstorm is expected to last? Do we have enough chopped wood for the fireplace? Do we—"

"Whoa, Leslie. Slow down. We'll get through this. Yes, the generator will work. Not sure how long the storm will last, but I'm hoping it will blow over in a few days. Yes, there's plenty of chopped wood, and yes, there are a few things you can help me do to get prepared."

"What?" she asked, and he could hear the eagerness to help in her voice.

"I'm going outside to put the car in the garage and to cover everything that needs to be protected. I'd like you to go around and gather the candles and matches. There's also batteries and mobile phone chargers in the closet at the end of the hallway."

"Okay."

"And since it's best not to run a generator overnight, we'll need to sleep in front of the fireplace for heat. That means we need to grab sleeping bags and blankets from that hall closet."

"Separate sleeping bags, of course."

"Of course," he said, somewhat annoyed she'd think he would take advantage of the situation.

"Give me a few minutes to get dressed and I'll get to everything right away."

An hour later, Sloan had done all the outside chores that needed to be done and had also brought in more wood for the fireplace. He'd noted that snow had already begun falling, and there was an increase in wind coming off the strait. He'd weathered harsh snowstorms before. You couldn't live in Alaska without having experienced a few; however, he had a feeling the one headed their way was a doozy.

As he bent down to add more wood to the box next to the fireplace, he could hear Leslie moving around in the kitchen. He couldn't help thinking about the fresh-showered Leslie who'd opened her bedroom door earlier. She had smelled good and had looked even better in her robe. First time he'd ever seen her in one. There was a time when she'd been comfortable wearing very little around him or nothing at all after a shower. He'd noted during one of his wood-toting trips into the house that she'd changed into a pair of jogging pants and a sweatshirt. She looked good in that, too.

"I pulled water bottles out of the cabinet and loaded them into one of the coolers filled with ice, Sloan."

He glanced up to see the subject of his thoughts standing beside him as he knelt in front of the fireplace. "That's a good idea," he said. "Glad you thought of it."

"Can you think of anything else you need me to do?" she asked.

He broke eye contact with her to poke at the fire. "I can't think of anything at the moment."

His phone rang, and he stood to pull it out of his back pocket. "Yes, Garth?"

"Regan and I are looking at the report on the weather

channel. Sounds like pretty bad weather headed your way. You're ready to hunker down for a while?"

"Ready as we'll ever be, Garth. Leslie and I will be just fine." He saw the lifting of Leslie's brow. Did it bother her that Garth knew she was there with him?

"Well, take care and I'll check on you guys tomorrow," Garth said, reclaiming Sloan's attention.

"The wind is pretty high outside. If you can't reach us, it might be the result of too much wind near the towers."

"Okay, I'll keep that in mind. I'll call and check on Walker, Bailey and the twins now. Tell Leslie hello."

Sloan ended the call with his brother and put the phone back into his pocket. "Garth says hello."

"He knows I'm here?" Leslie asked.

"Yes. Is there a reason why he shouldn't?"

She shook her head. "No, there's no reason. I'll make us some hot chocolate."

He nodded, appreciating that she remembered how much he liked the stuff. "Thanks. I have a feeling it's going to be a hot chocolate kind of night."

"I have that same feeling," she said, and then he watched her turn and walk off toward the kitchen.

Sloan rubbed his hand down his face. A turbulent Alaska snowstorm was headed their way, and of all things, he was stranded here alone with Leslie.

Fourteen

The sound of doors opening and closing brought Leslie awake. She lay there a moment and recalled the night before and how they'd prepared for the oncoming storm. Jumping out of bed, she raced to the window. A thick blanket of snow covered everything, and it was still coming down hard. She could barely see past where she knew the detached storage shed was. There was no doubt in her mind the temperature had dipped a lot lower than it had been when she'd finally gone to bed.

After pouring cups of hot chocolate for her and Sloan, they had then worked together to prepare things. She had followed him to the underground tunnel…at least that's what Sloan had called it. To Leslie it looked more like a man cave, with living quarters that included a flat-screen television, wet bar and a wall filled with a collection of bottles of wine.

To not overwork the generator, they had removed all electrical items that had been plugged in and made sure the doors were secured. Then they had carried more blankets and sleeping bags from one of the closets to the fireplace.

It had been close to two in the morning before they'd said good-night and gone to their individual bedrooms. She was certain that as soon as her head touched the pillow, she'd fallen asleep.

Moving away from the window, she returned to the bed and picked up her cell phone off the nightstand. She was glad it was still working. Sloan had warned her that even with the tower that had been installed, they might lose reception due to the strong winds. So far they hadn't, although it was taking longer than usual to make a connection to the weather app. The temperature had dropped ten degrees from where it had been when she'd gone to bed.

When she heard another door opening and then closing, she knew Sloan was already up. Glancing over at the clock, she saw it was almost nine and then realized she had forgotten to set the alarm. Her goal had been to be up by seven.

Moving quickly, she made the bed and then rushed to the bathroom for her morning shower, hoping Sloan had the coffee going.

Sloan's plan had been to return her to Wasilla today. Now they were stranded and had no choice but to make the most of it. Since the cabin was ready for the worst, he would probably start ignoring her. She noted he hadn't had a lot to say last night, even as they'd worked together to get things prepared.

A short while later, she had showered and dressed and was halfway to the kitchen when her nose picked up the aroma of coffee. Entering the kitchen, she saw him leaning against a kitchen counter sipping a cup. "Good morning, Sloan."

"Good morning, Leslie. I got your oatmeal ready."

"You didn't have to do that."

"I figured it was the least I could do since you prepared such a delicious breakfast yesterday. I recalled how much you like the stuff."

She went to the cabinet to grab a bowl, trying not to notice how good he looked in a pair of sweatpants with a matching sweatshirt that advertised Outlaw Freight Lines. He'd given her an OFL T-shirt years ago. It had been two sizes too large, and for years it had been the perfect sleep shirt. "You got up early."

"I doubt if I even slept. I lay there remembering stuff I should have done. So I got up and filled the tubs in the other bathrooms with water and went outside a few times to make sure the pipes were sufficiently covered."

"I see," she said, going to sit at the table after filling her bowl with oatmeal and grabbing a box of raisins. She was surprised when Sloan joined her at the table after refilling his cup.

"You started a trend with my siblings with that, you know."

She lifted a brow. "Oatmeal and raisins?"

"Yes. To this day it's Charm's favorite breakfast meal. She even has the old man eating it."

Leslie couldn't help but smile. "It's a good meal to add to anyone's diet. You even liked it yourself."

"Only because you liked it. There was a time I liked anything you liked."

She didn't know what to say to that, so she said nothing. Sloan in turn sat across from her and drank his coffee. He definitely appeared in a better mood this morning than he had been last evening.

As tempted as she was to glance over at him, she didn't. She couldn't. Nothing looked sexier than Sloan Outlaw when he needed a shave. Just thinking about tracing her palm across that bearded jaw had warmth seeping between her legs.

"Why didn't you return to Alaska after completing your studies at Howard, Leslie?" he broke into her thoughts to ask.

His question did make her look up. Did he really want to talk about that time in their past? If so, why? But since he'd asked, she would give him an answer. Even if it was the one she'd convinced herself she believed.

"Aunt Ella was getting up in age, and after she had a nasty fall that required months in rehab, Dad felt having me there with her was far more important than returning home."

There was no need to tell him that even after her aunt had fully recuperated, Leslie hadn't rushed back to Alaska because she'd still been suffering from a broken heart. It was only after she'd discovered the truth of Sarah's lies that she had given thought to returning home. She'd known at some point she couldn't move on without seeking Sloan out and apologizing for believing the worst about him.

He took another sip of his coffee and then asked, "Did you enjoy living in the nation's capital?"

She shrugged. "It was interesting and definitely different. It always amused me when the first drop in temperature caused people to panic. And their major snowstorms weren't anything compared to ours, that's for sure. But there were more nice days than not, and it's a beautiful place."

After taking a sip of her own coffee, she added, "I'm sure now that you have a brother who's a United States senator, you've visited there a lot."

"Not a lot, but enough. Jess has a nice place on the Potomac. And I agree about the weather. I also like its proximity to New York."

He didn't say anything for a while, and the room was quiet except for the howling of the wind and the rustling sound of snow falling. It wasn't even lunchtime yet, but the amount of snow falling made it appear dark outside, robbing them of their few hours of daylight. She was about to stand and take her empty bowl over to the sink when Sloan's next words stopped her.

"I need to know something, Leslie."

She could tell from the tone of his voice that whatever he needed to know was serious. Drawing in a deep breath, she asked, "What is it that you want to know, Sloan?"

He held her gaze. "How could you have thought I betrayed you with Sarah?"

A part of Sloan wanted to bite off his tongue for even asking, when he'd told himself over the years that he hadn't given a damn. He still didn't, but he figured at the moment, anything was better than his mind being preoccupied with that phone call he'd received from Cole before daybreak this morning, detailing new developments about Martin Longshire.

Just as Sloan had suspected, the man was trying to go after several of Sloan's companies with hostile takeover attempts. All it had taken was Sloan to make a couple of calls to his attorneys to turn the tables on Longshire once again. This time Sloan had left no doubt in anyone's mind, especially Longshire's, that compared to Sloan's wealth, Longshire was a pauper. Fearing Sloan would retaliate with a countertakeover, the stockholders of the Longshire Industries had demanded that Longshire step down as CEO immediately and take early retirement. It was basically the same type of ultimatum the board at Outlaw Freight Lines had given Bart.

"At the time it all seemed pretty clear," Leslie said, intruding into his thoughts. "You weren't returning my calls. And Sarah had what I thought was proof that you were texting and calling her and not me. The text messages she let me read were supposedly from you, begging her not to tell me what happened that night between the two of you, that it had been a mistake I didn't need to know about. I saw the text messages, Sloan. What was I supposed to believe?"

He tried to keep the anger from his voice when he said, "You should have believed that no matter what those text messages said, there was no way I could have slept with her."

"Even when you didn't return my call, I refused to believe it...until she provided proof."

"Those text messages and documentation of phone calls weren't proof of anything. Anyone can assign someone's name to a contact in their phone. Although it said the person making the calls and sending those text messages was me, it could have been made up."

"You think I didn't know that? That's why I tried calling you. But I couldn't reach you."

"The reason you couldn't reach me was because there was no reception at the cabin. That's why I didn't get your call." He rubbed his hand down his face and said, "But then, I can't fully place the blame solely on you, Leslie, since I should have told you."

He saw the confusion in her eyes. "You should have told me what?"

Sloan hesitated and then said, "That Sarah made a couple of passes at me before."

"What! And you didn't tell me about that?"

"I didn't tell you because I thought I had handled the situation. The first time she did it, I thought it was just her being flirty."

Leslie leaned over the table. "What exactly did she do?"

"She copped a feel of my ass. It happened at that birthday party Keosha gave for Tyler. I figured Sarah had had one drink too many. But then one day I stopped by your apartment and you weren't there. She invited me to come in and wait for you, claimed you had just made a quick trip to the store. That's when she tried coming on to me again. This time she was sober."

Leslie crossed her arms over her chest. "And just what did she do?"

He wished when she'd placed her hands across her chest the action didn't reveal a pair of full breasts he used to enjoy sucking.

"Sloan? What did she do?"

Bringing his focus back to her question, he said, "She tried to kiss me. It pissed me off, and I told her in no uncertain terms I didn't appreciate it and not to ever do it again. She began crying and apologized and said she wasn't sure what had gotten into her and promised it wouldn't happen again. She asked me not to mention it to you because she didn't want to lose your friendship."

Fire appeared in Leslie's eyes. "Well, she would have definitely lost my friendship. I could see you ignoring that time she was drunk, but not the time she tried to kiss you. You should have told me, Sloan."

He rubbed his hands down his face. "I told you why I didn't tell you. She started crying and apologized, Leslie. She said it wouldn't happen again, and I believed her. I saw her a number of times after that whenever I came to see you, and she never tried anything else. In fact, she went out of her way to avoid me. I had no reason to think she would have done it again or anything else remotely as devious."

"But she did, didn't she?" she snapped. "You should have told me. If you had told me, at least I would have been prepared for the lies. Thanks to you, I wasn't, and you had the audacity to get mad because I believed her?"

"Yes, I still felt you should have trusted me."

"But there was no reason for me not to believe her, Sloan. She probably felt emboldened knowing you hadn't told me about the incident, just like she'd asked you, which was why she decided to carry things further. Those text messages alone weren't what made me break things off with you and leave school. What hurt me more than anything was finding those panties."

Frowning, he sat up straight in his chair. "What panties?"

"*Her* panties. According to Sarah, that weekend I went out of town with the debate team, you offered her a ride home when you stopped by the café where she worked at closing time. Instead of taking her straight to our apartment, you took her somewhere for drinks. She claimed the two of you had a little too much to drink and decided to sober up in the parking lot instead of immediately driving home. She said one thing led to another, and the next thing she knew the two of you were making out in your car, right there in the parking lot."

"And you believed that?" he asked incredulously.

"I didn't until she told me where to find her panties. In your car. And I did find them, Sloan. They were just where she said they would be—stuffed under the cushion in the back seat."

Sloan stared at Leslie. This part about Sarah planting a pair of her panties in his car was news to him. How could she have done that when she'd never ridden in his car before? When he'd left for the cabin, he had left his car with Leslie. She had driven him to the airport and three days later was to use his car to drive herself there. She was to leave it parked at the airport when she caught the plane to join him in Kodiak. "If that's true, I have no idea how they got there. You had the car while I was gone. Did you ever give her a lift somewhere?"

Leslie shook her head. "No."

"Then she apparently got the keys without you knowing and put them there."

He watched her draw in a deep breath. "I guess that's what she did, Sloan. All I know is that night when I ran into her in LA, she'd been drinking, and that's when she told me the truth. She wanted me to know the text messages and panties had been used to deliberately break us up, and she even seemed pretty damn happy about it. Sarah showed no remorse at all and didn't say why she'd done it. I wish you had told me about her coming on to you. You didn't, and I was blindsided."

"You didn't have to leave town without telling me where you'd gone, Leslie. You could have confronted me about Sarah's lies when you saw me at the cabin."

She didn't say anything for a minute. "I felt I had to leave, Sloan. Sarah claimed the only reason she was finally leveling with me about what the two of you had done was because she'd missed her period, and if she was pregnant, the baby was yours."

"What!"

"Yes, that's what she told me. And just the thought of her having your baby was something I couldn't handle. I refused to stay around to find out if she was pregnant or not."

Sarah's lies had been deeper than he'd known. All this time he had assumed Leslie had left because of fake text messages and phone calls. "When did you find out she didn't have my baby?"

"I figured it was a false alarm when Keosha never mentioned anything whenever I talked to her."

"Did Keosha know the full extent of Sarah's lies?"

Leslie shook her head. "No. I never told her about anything but the text messages and phone calls. I made Keosha promise not to bring up your name in any of our conversations."

Sloan rubbed his hand behind his neck, feeling tension building there. He'd made Tyler and Redford promise the same thing about Leslie. The kitchen got quiet as she stood, and he watched her carry her bowl to the sink and rinse it out before putting it in the dishwasher. Then, without even looking at him, she walked out of the kitchen.

Sloan opened his mouth to call her back but then clamped it shut. She was right, and he couldn't argue the point. He should have told her about Sarah coming on to him. Because he hadn't, she hadn't known just what a vile person Sarah Olsen truly was.

Hell, he hadn't known. He'd honestly believed Sarah had regretted her actions. In the end, he'd been wrong. Sloan knew he couldn't fault Leslie for being taken in by the woman, because in the end, he had been fooled by her as well.

Fifteen

Leslie entered her bedroom, closing the door behind her, and began pacing the floor. She was upset knowing Sarah had come on to Sloan and he hadn't told her about it. Granted, that first time might have been due to her overdrinking like he'd assumed, but that second time should have set off red flags. Flags he should have told her about.

She glanced toward the door when she heard the knock. Knowing it was Sloan, she took her time moving to the door, not sure she wanted to see him. Opening the door, she raked her gaze over him as he stood with his hands shoved in the pockets of his jeans.

"What is it, Sloan?"

"Now it's me who owes you an apology, Leslie. I apologize."

She actually heard regret in his voice, and as she studied his features, she saw regret there as well. A part of her didn't want to accept his apology, but then, hadn't he accepted hers? And she couldn't dismiss the fact that he hadn't known about the panties or Sarah's claim of a possible pregnancy. Now that he did, she hoped he understood why she had been hurt to the point of needing to put distance between them. Why she had left school the way she had and forbidden her father to tell him where she'd gone.

Drawing in a deep breath, she said, "I accept your apology, Sloan. It seems we both could have handled things differently."

They hadn't, and it had cost them ten years. But then, maybe it hadn't been meant for them to be together for the long haul. Maybe it was only meant for him to be someone who would occupy her heart for a short while. That time had come and gone, and she knew it could never be recaptured again. She figured he knew it as well.

"Do you honestly accept my apology, Leslie?"

Leslie narrowed her gaze at him. "Just as much as you honestly accepted mine at the wedding."

It was easy to see her words had hit home, which let her know she'd been right. Although he'd told her he had accepted her apology that day, and while he'd reached out to her to help save her company, he'd still intended to exact his form of revenge as well. That made her wonder if helping to save her company had been as honorable as she'd assumed. Was there an ulterior motive for that as well?

She dismissed the thought. He might have not truly accepted her apology, but she believed getting her to sleep with him again was as far as he would have taken any retaliation he might have implemented. Nothing could convince her that helping to save her company wasn't aboveboard. He would not have taken things that far.

"Now, if you don't mind, there's a book I'd like to finish reading."

He nodded. "Do you want to cook dinner today, or would you prefer I take care of it?"

"I'll prepare something later."

"All right."

He walked off, and she closed the door. Leslie had barely made it across the room when the lights flickered and then they lost power for barely a minute. When the lights came back on, she knew the generator had kicked in. But like Sloan had told her, the generator had to be turned off at night. That meant to preserve heat, they would be sharing a spot in front of the fireplace tonight. She wasn't sure how she felt about that.

Leslie hoped the weather would improve by tomorrow and then she could be on her way. She didn't want to spend any more time than necessary with Sloan, and she was certain he felt the same about her.

Sloan looked up when Leslie entered the living room. "I see that we've lost power," she said.

"Yeah," he replied, following her gaze out the window. The high winds were causing sheets of ice to hit against it. It was like something out of a bad movie. He'd been expecting bad weather, but not to this degree. "I'm surprised the power lasted as long as it did," he said.

"Any idea how long this storm will last?"

He shook his head. "I don't have a clue. Even the tower isn't working, which means we can't send or receive calls. Last weather report I saw indicates we haven't been hit with the worst of it yet. To preserve the generator, we need to turn it off around seven."

"Then let me start dinner."

"And while you're doing that, I need to go outside and check around to make sure things are still covered."

"You're really going out in that, Sloan?" Leslie asked him in an incredulous voice, placing her hands on her hips.

He tried not to notice how good she looked standing there in her jeans and sweatshirt. "Yes. The wind is so high it might have blown something off, and I need to check while there's still a little daylight." He walked over to the hall closet and grabbed his coat, hat and gloves.

"How long will you be gone?"

Sloan was sliding into his coat when he met her eyes. "Probably no more than twenty minutes. I'll be back before you know it."

"Please be careful."

Was that concern he heard in her voice? He smiled at her, hoping that would assure her he would be fine. "I will," he said, putting on his gloves. "Do me a favor and have a cup of hot chocolate ready when I get back."

"I can do better than that. I'll also make sandwiches to go along with the hot chocolate."

He gave her a thumbs-up as he headed for the door, bracing himself against the wind that had gotten stronger over the past hours. One of Maverick's bright ideas had been to place heated planks in front of the door. That way snow wouldn't block the opening or closing of the door.

The moment he stepped outside, the freezing temperature cut him to the core. Shouldering his body against the snow and winds, he headed toward where the pipes were located to make sure they were still properly covered. It was cold as the dickens, and he figured if he thought about Leslie—specifically, how good she looked and how nice she smelled—it would warm up his insides somewhat.

After checking the pipes as well as several pieces of machinery to make sure they could continue to withstand the wind and snow, he was headed back toward the house when he noticed that a huge tree limb had blown to the ground, too close to the generator to suit him. Deciding to move the limb out of the way, he began tackling the job and discovered the limb was heavier than he'd thought. It ended up taking a lot longer than planned, but he had finally dragged it back to what he considered a safe distance.

He was about to head back toward the cabin when another huge tree branch came flying toward him like a missile. While ducking, he slipped on a patch of ice, and fell flat to the ground, the wind knocked out of him. It took him a few minutes to regain his strength enough to pull himself up to his knees. That's when he felt a pounding pain in his head and figured he hadn't moved quick enough. A part of the tree branch had struck the side of his head.

He was determined to get back to the cabin, though his head was hurting even more. Forcing himself to stand, he felt somewhat dizzy. When he felt himself getting lethargic, he pushed himself to continue walking as snow thickened even more around him.

Sloan knew the cabin should be close. If he could just ignore the cold and the pain, he would be fine. It was getting dark, and he wasn't even sure he was going in the right direction. The falling snow made it nearly impossible to see in front of him, but he had to keep moving and hoped he was going east and not west.

At that moment he wasn't sure of anything other than he was freezing cold and needed to get warm fast. He then thought of Leslie. The thought of never seeing her again shifted the pain from his head to his chest and close to his heart. He wasn't sure why, but it had.

He pushed his way forward, shivering from the inside out, yet determined to find his way back to Leslie.

Leslie stopped pacing long enough to check her watch. The house was quiet except for the sound of the sleet hitting the windows. It was getting dark. Sloan had said it wouldn't take him any longer than twenty minutes and he'd been gone close to an hour. Why hadn't he come back yet?

She glanced over at the cups of hot chocolate and the two sandwiches wrapped in cellophane. The hot chocolate had gone cold, and when he returned she would have to make some more. There was no problem if she had to do that, she just wanted him safe. Leaving the kitchen, she went to the living room window and practically pressed her face against it. She could barely see past the porch for all the snow that was falling. Glancing at her watch again, she decided to give Sloan ten more minutes. If he wasn't back by then, she would go looking for him. The wind had gotten louder, and the snow was falling more heavily.

Leslie began pacing again, getting more worried by the minute, especially when the wind outside sounded even more fierce. Deciding not to wait any longer, she went to the hall closet and pulled out her boots, coat, hat and gloves. She also grabbed a flashlight.

She was met with freezing temperatures the moment she opened the door, and she was tempted to go back inside. She could barely see beyond the porch, but she refused to turn around. To get her bearings for a moment, she huddled in the corner near the porch swing before pushing herself forward.

She called out for him but soon discovered her voice was drowned out by the sound of rushing winds. She hesitated before stepping off the porch, holding on to the rail as she did so. The wind was so strong she was convinced it could sweep her away easily, and the snow was coming down even more.

The flashlight helped. She wished Sloan had taken it with him. Since it had still been daylight when he'd left the cabin, he hadn't done so. Now it was dark. She stopped walking when she thought she heard a sound.

What had Sloan told her about bears? He claimed his property was bearproof and that most bears hibernated during the winter months. Even if the sound she'd heard wasn't a bear, it could be some other kind of animal. Like a moose. A very unfriendly moose. Or an even larger bison.

Refusing to give in to her fears, she began walking again, or else her feet would get frozen in place. Taking a chance, she called out to Sloan again in the loudest voice she could. Her eyebrows went up when she thought she heard a deep groan coming from the direction where she'd heard the sound earlier. She had a feeling what she'd heard wasn't a bear or any other animal but was Sloan. She called out to him again, and when she didn't hear anything, she braved the weather to move in that direction.

Moments later, she found him, leaning against the side of a tree. When she shined the flashlight on his face, she saw a bruise near his left eye. "Sloan! What happened?" she asked, reaching him.

"I got hit in the head with a flying branch and then I slipped and fell," he said in a shivering and slurred voice. "I need to get to the cabin. I'm almost frozen."

She saw that he was, and that wasn't good. "Lean against me, and we'll go back together."

"I'm too heavy, Leslie."

"No, you're not, so do what you're told, Sloan."

It must have been the tone of her voice. All she knew was that when she wrapped her arms around him, he leaned against her, and when they began walking, she slowed her pace to keep up with his steps. She then led him toward the area from where she'd come. She supported his weight and he supported hers as together they slowly moved toward the cabin.

"Are you sure we're going in the right direction?" he asked in a voice that shivered.

"Positive."

"Did you throw down bread crumbs?"

Leslie couldn't help but smile. In college, more than once, she'd gotten lost on campus while walking from one building to another. Jokingly, Sloan had suggested that she throw down bread crumbs to find her way. "Not this time."

Moments later, she said, "We're here."

"We're here?"

She could hear the surprise and gratitude in his voice. "Yes, Sloan, we're here."

Once they walked through the cabin door, Leslie knew her work had just begun. First thing she needed to do was get Sloan warmed up and then check his injuries. He had been out there a long time, and she needed to look for hypothermia and frostbite. She was grateful she'd been a Girl Scout back in the day.

They made it to the sofa. She checked the knot on his head and then raced to the kitchen for the first-aid kit. She made sure he took a couple of aspirin for the pain and determined there was no frostbite. But she needed to get him warm.

He assisted her in removing his wet clothes, and then she quickly removed hers. There was no time to be modest, since they'd both seen the other naked a number of times, although not recently. The important thing was getting dry as quickly as possible to share body heat.

Luckily for them the fire was blazing in the fireplace. Wrapping themselves in a sleeping bag and blankets, they lay down in front of it. She wished she could ignore the naked body plastered to hers that was shivering profusely. Hopefully, their bodies' heat would stop any hypothermia. She had taken a quick look at the knot on the side of his head. She needed to watch for any signs of a possible concussion, which meant waking him up periodically.

The feel of his hard body pressed against her back and his arms across her waist felt comforting. She didn't want to think of what the outcome could have been if she hadn't gone looking for him. From the way he was shivering, he was still cold, but the body pressed against hers was beginning to feel warm.

His arms tightened around her, and his body shifted slightly to whisper in her ear, "Thank you, Leslie."

The huskiness of his voice made certain parts of her tingle. "Don't mention it, Sloan."

She lay there, cuddled in his arms inside the sleeping bag, as they continued to share heat. She was facing the fireplace, and for the longest time she watched the blazing wood, trying to recall the last time she'd slept naked in his arms. It had been the day before he was to leave to come here and prepare this same cabin for their week during spring break. They had made love most of the night and again that morning before she'd taken him to the airport. That had also been the last time she'd seen him until she'd run into him at Tyler and Keosha's wedding.

Leslie thought about all they'd discovered about

what happened ten years ago, since being here. Lies she thought he'd known about, only to discover he hadn't. Their one accomplishment was realizing they both had contributed to their breakup. They had played right into Sarah's hands, and she felt herself getting angry just thinking about it.

As for Sloan, she had no idea what he was thinking. Was he also remembering the last time their bodies had fit this snugly? When she heard Sloan's even breathing, she knew he had drifted off to sleep, which meant he wasn't thinking at all.

Leslie wished she could say the same about herself, but she was thinking and doing a lot of it. What if she hadn't gone looking for Sloan? What if he'd been injured far worse than he had? What if he'd gotten frostbite and needed extreme medical care and she couldn't give it to him or expect anyone to come out in this weather? What if...

She closed her eyes, not wanting to think about all the things that could possibly have gone wrong. Instead, she focused on all the things that had gone right. He was back in the cabin and safe.

They might have been apart for ten years, but she knew some things hadn't changed. And that included her love for him.

Yes, she still loved Sloan, and it had taken almost losing him to make her realize that. She also knew he'd seen her leaving him ten years ago as no different than the way his own mother had deserted him. He had shared with Leslie how he'd felt about his mother's desertion, how it had affected him, although he knew he'd had a better life without her.

And Leslie knew he couldn't trust her after what had happened ten years ago. More than anything she wished she had more time with Sloan, but she knew that wouldn't be the case. There was no doubt in her mind, when the weather cleared up he would be taking her back to Wasilla as planned. She knew it, and although she wished otherwise, she accepted it. She'd appreciate having him here with her for as long as the weather lasted.

Sixteen

Sloan slowly opened his eyes as his gaze skimmed over the woman who slept snuggled beside him in the sleeping bag. She lay pressed close to him in the spoon position with one of his legs thrown over her thigh. She smelled good and was very much naked. But then, so was he. How did this happen when Leslie had made it pretty damn clear they would have separate sleeping bags? More importantly, how could he have slept naked with her all through the night and not...

Suddenly, memories of the day before flooded his mind. Leslie had awakened him periodically due to a possible concussion. He even recalled her shoving more aspirin and water down his throat each time she did so. And then he'd dozed back off.

Clearly his mind had been fuzzy for him not to fully

realize Leslie was sleeping with him naked. He knew the sharing of body heat was the best way to ward off hypothermia, but he honestly would not have thought she would have gone that far. But she had. The proof was that she was sleeping in his arms without a stitch of clothing on.

Forcing that thought from his mind, he glanced across the room to look out the window. From the sound of it, the wind was still howling, and it seemed snow was still coming down hard. The timer had kicked on, and the generator was back on for the next twelve hours.

"You're awake."

He looked down at Leslie, and all kinds of sensations floated around in his chest. He'd forgotten how sexy a just-waking-up Leslie looked. "Yes, I'm awake."

She shifted to face him. "How do you feel? Does your head hurt?"

Before he could answer, she reached up to place the back of her hand against his forehead. He recalled that was something else she'd done a number of times during the night, to check his temperature. As far as how he felt, it wasn't *this* head that was pounding, but the one between his legs pressing against her. There was no way she couldn't feel his leg or his erection…with the both of them being naked and all.

"No, I'm fine. Actually, I'm feeling a lot better," he said, trying to sound convincing.

"It's time for more aspirin," she said, reaching to grab the pill bottle off the coffee table, along with a bottle of water. Her movement shifted their bodies, but he still managed to keep his leg over hers. And it seemed his erection was determined not to go anywhere, either.

Shifting his body somewhat, he took the aspirin and water, downing both while holding her gaze. He handed the glass back to her. "I guess I'll live," he said, grinning.

"You better. Now I'll go fix that hot chocolate you didn't get to enjoy yesterday. I trashed the sandwiches but will be glad to make you an omelet."

Forget about whatever meal he'd missed yesterday. His thoughts were on what he could enjoy this morning. Right at this moment. "Can you wait on the hot chocolate and omelet a minute? There's something I need to ask you."

A wary look appeared in her eyes. Did she honestly think he would ask her for sex? If she recalled, whenever they made love, it had been because the sexual chemistry between them had been overwhelming. He was attracted to her now, and the sexual chemistry was strong. However, he wasn't sure it was mutual.

"What do you want to ask me, Sloan?"

He drew in a deep breath. "I need to know what made you come looking for me last night."

She broke eye contact with him and glanced out the window, not saying anything for a moment. "You were gone longer than you said you would be. I got worried. It was either go see what was taking you so long or pace the floor worrying even more. I chose the former."

"But the weather had turned into a blizzard, Les." He then realized he'd called her what he'd normally called her while they'd been together. She had been Les and not Leslie.

"I know that. I also knew you were out there in it. I tried to convince myself that you could take care of yourself, but I also knew with the amount of wind blowing and snow coming down that anything could have happened."

She paused again before saying, "Chances are, you would have made it back to the cabin, but I couldn't risk the chance you would not have."

He tried not to concentrate on the sadness he heard in her voice and saw in her eyes. Instead, he concentrated on her mouth and in doing so was reminded of just how it tasted. "Not sure if I would have made it back. My head was hurting, and it was getting harder and harder to make my body move because I was so cold. Hell, I wasn't even sure I was going in the right direction. I regret you put your own life at risk, but I'm damn glad you were there when I needed you."

"Just like you were there for me and my company when I needed you, Sloan," she said softly.

Her words made him realize that they'd been there for each other when it had mattered the most. He didn't want to think what would have been the outcome if he'd been at the cabin alone as originally planned and the snowstorm hit. Nor did he want to think what would have happened to her and her company if Redford hadn't told him what was going on. The potential outcome of either made him shiver.

"You're still cold. I'd better go and get that hot chocolate going," she said, shifting to get up and reaching for her clothes.

"Don't go yet," he said, not ready for any distance to be put between them or their bodies.

She glanced over at him. Their gazes held and then, as if she'd just noticed his erection pressing against her thigh, she said, "You do know the only reason why we're naked in this sleeping bag together, right?"

He nodded. "Yes. Because I needed your body's heat last night." He inched his mouth closer to hers and then said, "Only problem is, I still need your body's heat, Les. But now I need it for a totally different reason."

And then he leaned in and kissed her.

Leslie knew she should break off the kiss, pull herself out of Sloan's arms and put on clothes and head for the kitchen. But on the other hand, she didn't want to do any of those things. All she could think about was that she could have lost him. She forced the thought from her mind that she really didn't have him, because that didn't matter. No matter how he felt about her, she knew how she felt about him, and that was what mattered to her.

So instead of pulling away, she settled into the arms holding her while he was giving her one hell of a hot, deep and thorough kiss. It was a kiss that had her sliding her arms around his neck and kissing him back like her life depended on it.

Every muscle in her body seemed to come alive beneath the onslaught of his mouth. It was different than the kiss they'd shared in North Pole under the Northern Lights. There was something more seductive about the way his mouth took hers, gliding his tongue over hers like he thought it belonged to him. She then felt the tightness of his arms around her as the kiss blazed heat into her.

Somehow during the kiss, they had wiggled their way out of the sleeping bag and were naked on top of it. When she felt his palm caress her nipples, she couldn't hold back her whimper. In the deep recesses of her mind, she thought about all the other times they'd made love, but then she pushed them away. This was a different time. Same man. What she felt now was even more powerful. Sloan was kissing her long, he was kissing her hard. He had her heart pounding in desire so strong she felt herself drowning in it.

Last night, she'd accepted the realization she still loved Sloan. And now in the brightness of a new day, she knew she had never wanted Sloan Outlaw more than she did at that very moment. She wanted him and she needed him. It didn't matter that there was no future for them, or that whenever the weather cleared, he would still be taking her home. At that moment, she needed the ultimate in sexual pleasure that only Sloan could give her.

Panting heavily, she broke off the kiss, and their eyes locked while they both fought to get their breathing under control. The eyes staring back at her were dark, hot and filled with more yearning than she'd ever seen in them. This Sloan was ten years older, which meant over the years his desire, wants and needs had changed. Could she handle this more experienced Sloan? A more important question to ask was…would she be enough for him?

He took her wrist and brought it to his lips to place a kiss there. Still holding her gaze, and as if he'd read her thoughts, he said, "I want you, Leslie. I want you more than I've wanted any woman. That hasn't changed."

His words managed to calm her rattled nerves and appease her unsettled mind. Yet heat flared through her. Was she imagining things, or were their heartbeats in sync? She could tell him that she wanted him more than she had any other man, and that since him there had been no one else. But then she figured that was something he didn't need to know right now—or possibly ever.

"Are you sure, Sloan? You said you wanted me for Christmas, but we both know when you said it, it was for all the wrong reasons."

"I still want you for Christmas, but now it's for all the right reasons. What I should be asking you is whether you want me. Do you, Les?" he asked while trailing the tip of his finger down her jaw to her throat.

His touch generated a hunger deep within her, and the eyes staring back at her were expressing a desire that was making her heart rate increase. Why was he calling her Les? Did he not know doing so brought back memories of a time when just the sound of him calling her that would send her body into a tailspin of longing?

"Les?"

"Yes, I want you, Sloan."

"And not because of the near trauma of last night, right?"

What was he asking her? Just what was he trying to get her to say? Maybe she should be the one asking him that, given the feel of the huge erection pressing against her thigh. "Do you want me because of last night?" She needed to know the answer to that as much as he did.

He shook his head. "No, that's not what this is about for me, and I don't want it to be what it's about for you, either."

She nibbled on her bottom lip, nearly too afraid to ask, but she did so anyway. "Then what should it be about?"

His fingers reached up to gently stroke her chin, and his touch nearly sent her over the edge. It increased the heat spreading through her body. "It's about two people who once cared a lot for each other, who allowed someone to destroy what they had. It's about them still desiring each other and wanting each other for the right reason."

She thought on his words and noted he wasn't making any promises of anything after today. "And what reason is that, Sloan?"

"Now that we both know the truth of what happened ten years ago, that truth has set us free."

Sloan meant the words he'd spoken to Leslie. They were now free of lies, anger and resentment. However, from the way she was staring at him, he could tell she didn't fully comprehend the magnitude of what that meant.

He saw the guarded eyes staring at him. The only way he knew to help her understand was to show her, and it would be a demonstration that removed any doubts—on both their parts—as to where they would go from here. Hopefully, by the end of the storm, they both would know.

His gaze swept over her, and he could actually feel the whoosh of blood racing through his veins. He glanced back at her when he heard the change in her breathing. At that moment he knew she felt as drawn to him as he was to her. Holding her gaze, he asked, "What do we have to lose by trying, Les?"

He swooped his mouth down on hers. He took his time, savoring her, enjoying the taste it had taken him years to get over. Now he wondered if he really had.

Angling his head to explore her mouth the way he wanted, he moaned when her tongue met his. They explored each other's mouths with an urgency that was overwhelming yet at the same time welcoming. He felt her hand touch his back, and the warmth of it soothed him yet at the same time felt hot. He disengaged their mouths for a quick breath and then latched back on to her mouth, returning for more.

By the time he broke off the kiss again, the room seemed to vibrate around them, and she quivered. He felt somewhat dizzy, and it had nothing to do with the blow to the head he'd received last night. It had everything to do with Leslie. Only Leslie. Her mouth had the ability to send a strong man keeling over with need.

Sloan drew in a deep breath, and when he did so, it included her scent, one that was uniquely her. He'd missed it. He breathed her in again, while holding her gaze with his. When he saw her nibble on her bottom lip, he knew what she was doing and why. Initially she'd been reluctant to tell him what she wanted whenever they made love, but over time she had gotten bolder. Now it seemed she didn't feel quite comfortable doing so. He intended to remedy that.

"How bad do you want me, Les? I need to know if it's as bad as I want you."

Her expression turned serious, and when she swallowed, he saw how fast the pulse was moving in her throat. "How bad do you want me, Sloan?"

He reached out and brushed the pad of this thumb against her cheek. "I want you so bad that I ache for you all over, especially in my groin."

He saw the flare of heat in her eyes. Instead of nibbling on her lips, she swiped her tongue across them before saying, "And I want you so bad that I ache for you, too. Especially between my legs."

It wasn't what she'd said but rather how she'd said it—in a tone of voice he hadn't heard in years. It was a tone filled with a desire he'd come to recognize and appreciate because it had always been just for him. Recognizing that tone had him easing up on his knees to open a secret compartment to the coffee table to pull out a condom packet.

At one time there had been five sexually active Outlaw brothers, and most didn't come to the cabin alone. It was understood there would be times when they might not make it to the bedroom, and it was always better to be safe than sorry. With Garth and Cash married off now, that meant it was up to Sloan, Jess and Maverick to replenish the supply whenever needed.

Although Sloan had never brought a woman here, he'd had no problem donating to the cause to make sure there were always plenty on hand. Now he was glad he had. He knew Leslie's eyes were on him while he sheathed himself. She'd once told him she loved seeing him do this part and would often get turned on by it. He wanted her more than turned on. He wanted her hot, eager and filled with need.

Sloan then returned to her, placed his body in position over hers while leaning on his elbows to stare down at her, totally overjoyed at what was to come. "I'm still a foreplay kind of guy, Leslie. You know what that means, right?"

She nodded and licked her lips again before she said, "Yes, I know."

He smiled and whispered, "So enjoy me like I plan to enjoy you."

Seventeen

There was so much desire in Sloan's eyes that it would have given her pause if Leslie thought it wasn't a mirror of her own. She didn't want to entertain all the questions that were bombarding her mind. The main one continued to be, just where would this lead?

At the moment, the only destination was pleasure. One part of her knew she needed to put a stop to this madness when she didn't have answers, but another part of her knew she was too swept away to do anything about it. She hadn't been consumed with this much passion in years. Ten years, to be exact. Now she was ready, and there was no doubt in her mind that Sloan Outlaw would deliver. She had watched him. She had seen the size of his erection when he'd donned the condom. It was hard and primed, and he wanted her.

She had been tempted to reach out and touch it, encircle her hands around it to show him just how much she wanted him, too. It no longer mattered to her that even after they'd made love, nothing would change between her and Sloan. When the weather improved, he would still take her home. The only difference was that she would be taking memories of this time with her. A day of pleasure in his arms, at this cabin and in front of a warm and inviting fireplace.

All thoughts suddenly left her mind when she felt him gently caressing her womanly folds, then spreading them open. She closed her eyes when she felt one finger, then another, ease inside her. He began stirring around inside her to the point where she couldn't hold back a moan even if she'd wanted to.

Leslie moaned when his mouth spread hot, wet kisses along her inner thighs. And then when the tip of his tongue massaged her, she instinctively moved her hips. He grabbed her hips to keep her in place when his tongue penetrated her and then consumed her with a greed that rocked her to the very core. Passion speared through her entire body, making her fully aware of what he was doing, how he was doing it and how much she had missed him doing it.

She felt him nudge her legs farther apart as his mouth and tongue continued to drive her over the edge, taking her breath away. He was behaving worse than the last name he bore. *Outlaw*. He was more like a desperado, a bandit of the most merciless kind.

He must have felt her body getting ready to explode, because he moved his tongue in such a way that her muscles tightened just seconds before she cried out his name.

"Sloan!"

Opening her eyes, she stared at him, and from the look in the eyes staring back at her, she knew he wasn't through with her yet. He proved her right when he began licking her body, moving up toward her chest, stopping briefly to pay homage to her navel. She knew where he was headed and tried bracing herself for the impact of how it would be when he got there. However, nothing could have prepared her for the feel of one of her nipples being sucked into his mouth. What he was doing to her breasts swamped all her senses, almost making her come again. Didn't he remember how sensitive her breasts were?

There was no doubt in her mind that he remembered, and he was letting her know he not only remembered but also planned to take advantage of that fact. He proved her right when he latched on to a nipple and she released a deep groan. The wet heat from his tongue devoured her. He acted as if she was the best thing he'd had in his mouth in a long time.

Thrumming sensations started at the soles of her feet and began moving upward. Recognizing the feeling for what it was, she strained her inner muscles to keep it from happening and discovered there was no use. She couldn't hold back. After inhaling a deep gulp of air, she cried out his name again, but he didn't let her go until the final moan had escaped her lips. Leslie was convinced Sloan was trying to kill her, but if she died it would be a pleasurable death.

"The best is yet to come, baby," he whispered, covering her body with his. "Open your eyes and look at me, Les."

Leslie opened her eyes and looked at him. That's how it had always been whenever they made love. He'd wanted them to be looking at each other the moment he entered her. The thought that he wanted to do things the same way filled her with so much pleasure. She fought back telling him that she loved him. It would not serve any purpose, since he didn't feel the same way. The last thing she wanted was for him to regret what they were sharing. No promises had been made. She was getting what she wanted and so was he.

"Are you concentrating on us, Les?" he asked as he sank into her, going deeper than she'd known him to ever go before.

"Yes, I'm concentrating on us," she whispered.

"Good."

He began moving, thrusting in and out. Slow at first and then faster. When she pushed her hips up to meet his downward thrusts, he pounded into her harder and deeper. The only sound in the room, other than the logs crackling in the fireplace, was their rapid breathing as he continued to drive harder and harder into her. And if that torture wasn't enough, he leaned close and licked her face, starting with her cheeks and ending on her bottom lip.

When she opened her mouth to let out a scream, he captured it with his lips at the same moment his hands grabbed her hips to rock deeper inside her. When he finally released her mouth, she screamed as another orgasm ripped through her. He didn't stop but kept going, thrusting as if he hadn't gotten enough and didn't intend to stop until he did.

When he cried out her name, the sound thundered in her ears louder than the sound of a building being blasted to smithereens. Numerous spasms racked their bodies while their cries of pleasure mingled, lengthened. Yet he didn't let her go. Although he shifted his body so his weight wouldn't hurt her, he continued to hold her while still filling her completely.

She felt satisfied and didn't mind him holding her close. At that moment she couldn't think of anywhere else she would rather be.

The snowstorm wasn't letting up. But then, Sloan thought, neither was he as he slid into Leslie's body again. Making love that first time and enjoying the experience of lying there with their bodies still intimately connected had only fueled his desire. He'd wanted more, and he was getting it.

Earlier they had taken the time, finally, to go into the kitchen for lunch, since they'd made love through breakfast. Then afterward they had returned to their place in front of the fireplace to make love all over again. Watching her undress had nearly brought out the beast in him, and he'd ended up licking every inch of her body, determined to satisfy a different kind of hunger.

Gazing deep into her eyes as he thrust hard inside her, establishing that perfect rhythm their bodies seemed to know and accept. It seemed to be an agreement not spoken aloud that they might as well continue through the rest of the day and well into the night. There was no reason for them not to when the desire was strong and condoms were plentiful.

So here he was, between the most gorgeous pair of legs to walk this earth, while he held tight to her perfect little ass and thrust hard into her with long, measured strokes. Gazing into her eyes told him she was feeling everything he was feeling. More than anything, he wanted her to know just how much he needed what she was unselfishly sharing with him.

As he stared into her dark, intense eyes, memories flooded him of other times they'd made love. They'd been young, probably hadn't known what they'd been doing most of the time, but now, with every downward thrust into her body, he knew exactly what he was doing. He was in a perfect place. Inside her. Feeling her inner muscles clench him, trying to hold him hostage while he stroked in and out. Hell, he could even feel his erection inside her getting larger. Her moans meant she felt it, too.

Leaning closer, he broke eye contact to kiss her neck, licked her there, rubbed his nose against her, loving her scent, the taste of her skin, every single thing about her.

"Sloan…"

He lifted his head to look into her eyes again, not missing a beat, not a single stroke, as he continued to thrust hard into her body. Hers seemed to stretch for him, taking all he had, and that made his erection harden even more. Made the magnitude of his arousal for her that much stronger.

Sloan could feel it about to happen but refused to

let it. He wasn't going over the edge unless Leslie went with him. He increased the pace and knew the minute she came; he heard it in her scream, felt it in her body as it jerked and quivered beneath his. It was only when she came that he let loose inside her. He felt her. He felt so damn good. Great. Totally satisfied to the nth degree.

When the tremors eased from both their bodies, he leaned in and kissed her, needing her to know how much he'd enjoyed making love to her and how good he felt. Easing off her, he drew her naked body into his arms and enjoyed the feel of her cuddled with him. Wrapping his arms around her waist as if he'd never let her go, he closed his eyes to sleep.

Eighteen

"It's finally let up," Leslie said as she stood at the window looking out. The wind had died down, and it was no longer snowing.

"After nearly three days of nonstop snow, it's about time, don't you think?" Sloan said, coming to stand beside her.

She looked over at him. Those snow days had been wonderful for her. Not just the time they'd spent either in bed, making out in front of the fireplace or in the shower, but the time they spent together, talking over hot chocolate or their meals, or just curled up together on the sofa.

He told her about several of his business ventures and the plans he had for them. He also told her about the call he'd gotten three days ago concerning Martin

Longshire, and what Sloan had to finally do to show
the man he meant business. Although she regretted it
had to come to Longshire being asked to step down, she
knew over time he would have gotten worse. The man
didn't know the meaning of cutting losses and moving
on. Sloan also told her more about his Westmoreland
cousins and through him she got to know them better.
The one thing they hadn't talked about, and what she
wasn't sure about, was what would happen with them.

"Now that it has stopped snowing, does that mean
you're ready to take me back to Wasilla, Sloan?" she
asked, wanting to know, since as far as she knew his
plans hadn't changed.

He turned to face her, reaching out to hold her around
the waist. "Do you still want to leave?"

Leslie raised her chin. "If I recall, my leaving was
your idea. You couldn't wait for me to be gone."

"But that was before…"

When his voice trailed off and he didn't finish what
he was about to say, she decided to finish it for him.
"Before what? Our two-day sex marathon?"

He frowned. "It was more than that, and you know
it."

"Do I, Sloan? I don't recall you saying it was more."

"Well, I'm saying it now," he said, turning to walk
off.

That wasn't good enough for Leslie. "Tell me how it
was more than that, Sloan."

He stopped walking and turned to her. "Why do you
want to get into this now, Leslie? Why can't we continue to enjoy the moment?"

She bit her bottom lip to hold back saying what she really wanted to say. Instead, she said, "I guess there's no reason we can't, Sloan."

"Good."

Leslie doubted he knew how much his words hurt. There were a number of reasons why they couldn't continue to enjoy the moment without them deciding where things went with them from here. His words basically let her know that what she'd assumed was true. Over the past couple of days, they had been making up for all those years they'd been apart, but with no real plan in place to move forward together beyond this week. All she'd been was a bed partner for him during the storm. She'd suspected it, but she had hoped he'd eventually see things differently. Although he'd admitted he was just as much to blame as she was for their breakup, he wasn't ready for a reconciliation. The only thing he was ready for was sex.

"Now that the roads appear clear, I need to drive over to Walker's. I talked to him earlier, and he has an extra fuse that I need for the electric box in the underground tunnel. Will you be okay here until I get back?"

She plastered a smile on her face. "Yes, of course, I'll be fine."

Twenty minutes later, Leslie stood in front of the window and watched as Sloan drove away. He hadn't even bothered inviting her to go with him. It wasn't like she and Walker had never met. Besides, she would have loved to have met Walker's wife and seen their twins. Evidently Sloan didn't consider Leslie worthy of doing either.

At that moment, she knew what she needed to do. Grabbing her cell phone off the table, she was glad it was working again. It didn't take long to arrange a car service to take her to the airport. A part of her refused to think that she was doing the exact same thing she'd done ten years ago, which was to run away without confronting him. In a way that might be true but this time it wasn't about a lie she believed. It was about the truth she knew. She loved him but he didn't love her.

Accepting that truth, she had to pack and be ready when the car arrived and hope she was gone by the time Sloan returned.

It was obvious that he wasn't ready to say one way or the other if she meant anything to him, so she had to assume she didn't. Ten years ago, the only way she'd gotten over him had been to make a clean break. To protect her heart, she had no choice but to leave him once again.

Sloan entered the cabin. He'd been gone way longer than expected, because part of the roof on Walker's barn had collapsed from the weight of the snow. Sloan had helped with temporary repairs until the roofer could get there tomorrow.

He noticed that although it had gotten dark outside, there were no lights on inside the cabin. Was Leslie in her room reading now that power was fully restored? He'd sent her a text message letting her know he would be delayed because he was helping Walker with the roof.

Bailey had raked him over the coals for not inviting Leslie along, saying she would have loved to have met her. When he'd told Bailey he hadn't brought Leslie because there was no reason for the two of them to meet, it had suddenly occurred to him what his words had meant.

Those words hadn't been true, and he'd known it.

When he'd left for Walker's, he'd been deliberately running away from emotions he hadn't been ready to face. Emotions Leslie had forced him to face. He couldn't help but recall bits and pieces of their conversation earlier…

Does that mean you're ready to take me back to Wasilla, Sloan?

Do you still want to leave?

If I recall, my leaving was your idea. You couldn't wait for me to be gone.

But that was before…

Before what? Our two-day sex marathon?

It was more than that, and you know it.

Do I, Sloan? I don't recall you saying it was more.

Well, I'm saying it now.

Tell me how it was more than that, Sloan.

Sloan hadn't told her because at the time he couldn't. Instead, he had found an excuse to leave. To escape by putting distance between them—that had given him a chance to think and accept a few things.

Now he could tell her what he should have told her during those two days they'd been making love. What he should have told her when she had confronted him earlier before he left the cabin to go to Walker's. He could tell her that making love to her was more than just a sexual marathon, because he loved her.

She had made him realize that he hadn't stopped loving her. That's what had made him protect her from the likes of Martin Longshire. What had made him want to spend time with her at the cabin. And what had gotten him to finally see that those plans he'd had for bringing her to the cabin had been made for the wrong reasons, what had made him see that taking her back to Wasilla was the right thing to do.

Now he needed to tell her why taking her back to Wasilla was *not* the right thing to do. He needed the rest of the week to show her their time together meant more to him than sex. It was about loving her unconditionally. Wanting a life with her. Sharing everything with her. Having children with her. He smiled at the thought of a little girl as beautiful as her mother.

He was about to head down the hall, eager to see Leslie, when he realized Leslie had removed all the Christmas decorations and had placed them in a box beside the tree. Why had she done that now when they had two more days to spend at the cabin?

The hairs on the back of his neck stood up as he moved toward the tree. When he got closer, he spotted the note hanging on one of the branches. Snatching it off, he read it.

Sloan, I am returning to Wasilla. Thanks for a wonderful time at the cabin. I hope you got what you wanted for Christmas.
Leslie

Sloan crumbled the paper in his hand as he headed for his bedroom to pack. If Leslie Cassidy thought she could take off and run away from him a second time, then he intended to prove her wrong.

He was in the middle of packing when his cell phone went off. He quickly pulled it out of the pocket of his jacket, hoping it was Leslie, but sighed in disappointment when he saw it was Cole. "What's going on, Cole?"

"Calling for two reasons. First, I wanted to make sure you're okay. We all heard about that massive snowstorm and were concerned when we couldn't get through to you, Walker and Bailey."

"We survived," he said, deciding not to mention his accident. Just thinking about it made him once again appreciate that Leslie had been there with him.

"Good to hear it. The other reason I'm calling is about Martin Longshire."

Sloan stopped packing and released a frustrated sigh. "Please don't tell me Longshire has refused to step down and I have to take away his company."

Cole chuckled. "No, that's not it. I understand that, although he's not happy about it, he will retire and has plans to move back to Paris."

"Good riddance. So, what's up with the man?"

"While checking him out, I came across a few things that warranted further digging. There's something I found rather interesting, and I'm not sure you know about it."

"And what's that?" Sloan asked as he resumed packing. He placed the call on speaker so he could move around as he threw items into his luggage.

"Did you know that a few years ago, Longshire was some young woman's secret sugar daddy?"

Sloan continued packing. "Why would that be of any interest to me, Cole?"

"Because the woman was Sarah Olsen, Leslie Cassidy's roommate."

Sloan went still. "Damn."

Nineteen

"You deserted Sloan Outlaw a second time, Leslie?"

Leslie rolled her eyes. Leave it to Carmen to get dramatic. "Trust me, he got just what he wanted from me. If you recall, he wanted *me* for Christmas."

She wouldn't bother mentioning that she'd gotten what she'd wanted from him, too, even when she hadn't realized she had wanted it or needed it. All it had taken was a day in Sloan's arms to make her realize just what she'd missed the past ten years. To be honest, she hadn't gotten enough of him.

"And what if he comes after you?"

"He won't, since he has no reason to do so. Besides, it's been almost two days and I haven't heard from him. Not even a phone call." She had received a text message on the day she'd left letting her know he would be returning to the cabin later than expected, because he was helping Walker. She hadn't responded to the text because she'd been busy packing.

"You know what they say, Carmen. Out of sight means out of mind. I figure since he is my business partner I'll eventually see him at some point after the office opens in January."

"And you're okay with that?"

She opened her mouth to lie and discovered she couldn't. This was Carmen. Her best friend. The woman who knew all her secrets. Most of them, anyway. Carmen knew how much Leslie had loved Sloan before and probably suspected she loved him now. "It doesn't matter. Sloan made it clear all we were sharing was sex this time."

"But you said he told you it was more."

"Yes, he did say that, but he couldn't tell me how it was more, so what he said doesn't count, Carmen."

"Well, at least the two of you know the extent of Sarah Olsen's deceit."

"Yes, now I know what he didn't know."

"I wonder how Sarah can live with herself after what she did."

Leslie rolled her eyes. "You saw her at that nightclub, and you heard how she bragged about it. She might have been drinking, but she didn't have any remorse then and I doubt she has any now." Leslie glanced at her watch. "Look, Carmen, I need to go finish up my laundry."

"All right. And you still haven't made any plans for the holidays?"

"Nope," she said, looking at the Christmas tree. "I plan to spend quiet time here."

"You know you're welcome to join me in Atlanta at my sister's. She would love seeing you again. And Elan received that package you sent to him. He can't wait to open it on Christmas Day."

"I'm glad he got it. Thanks for the invite, but I'll be okay."

A few hours later, she had finished laundry and taken a bath. She had changed into her Christmas pj's she'd gotten from Carmen last year. She'd even taken the time to make Christmas brownies and a batch of sugar cookies. The house was filled with the aroma of baked goods, and she liked it.

Leslie headed for the stairs to grab her e-reader and finish the book she'd begun reading at the cabin when she heard the doorbell. She went still, having an idea who was at the door. There was a reason her body was beginning to tingle all over.

Deciding to ignore the bell, she was about to go upstairs as heavy knocks sounded on the door. Frowning, she decided to answer it to see what Sloan could possibly want. When she snatched the door open, a bouquet of red roses stared her in the face, but she recognized the hand holding them. "What do you want, Sloan?"

He lowered the flowers and said, "Now that's a loaded question, Les."

Her frown deepened. "No, it's not, and the name is Leslie to you."

Instead of addressing what she'd said, he asked, "May I come in so we can talk?"

"Why?"

"I think we need to clear up a few things. Besides, it's cold as the dickens out here."

"So? You like the cold."

He shrugged. "I *liked* the cold. That episode at the cabin has changed my mind about that. Now can I come in so we can talk?"

Deciding she didn't want to freeze while standing in the doorway talking to him, she moved aside to let him in.

He glanced over at the tree. "Nice tree."

She crossed her arms over her chest. "You've seen it before, Sloan."

"Yes, I have." He sniffed the air. "Something smells good. You're baking?"

"Yes." She needed him to say whatever he'd come there to say so he could leave. Seeing him standing in her foyer, looking yummy enough to eat, wasn't good.

"Do you mind if I remove my coat, Leslie?"

Deciding not to be impolite, especially when he'd called her by her full name, she said, "You can give it to me and I'll hang it up. I'm sure whatever you have to say won't take long." After putting his coat in the closet, she walked off toward the living room, and he followed.

Leslie offered him the wingback chair, and she sat down on the sofa. "So what do you want to talk about, Sloan?"

He leaned forward, and when he did so, his jeans tightened across thighs she remembered riding. "First, I have a question for you about Sarah Olsen."

She frowned, wondering why he would bring her up. "What about Sarah?"

"Did you know that while the two of you were roommates, more specifically, during the time you and I were together, that Sarah and Martin Longshire were involved in an affair?"

She knew her expression must have shown her shock as she leaned forward in her seat as well. "Are you kidding me?"

He shook his head. "No, I'm not kidding you."

"Do you think he had anything to do with aiding and abetting our breakup?"

Sloan held her gaze. "I know he did. I paid Sarah a visit, and she confessed to everything."

"Was she sober?"

He nodded. "Yes. She was also desperate to save her job but was fired anyway."

Leslie leaned back in her seat. "I don't understand."

He leaned back in his chair as well. "You know the old saying what comes around goes around?"

"Yes."

"After discovering Sarah was involved with Longshire, I had Cole research her. Imagine my surprise to find out that she's living in LA and had a real cushy sales and marketing position with a film company where I'm a silent partner. Imagine *her* surprise when she walked into the conference room to find me sitting there."

"And?"

"And she confessed to everything she did to break us up and said Longshire paid her to make sure we ended our relationship. He figured hurting you was a way to get back at your father and your deceased mother."

Leslie stood, too angry to sit, and began pacing. "I had nothing to do with what happened between my parents and Longshire. He had no right to go after me."

"No. Just like he had no right to go after the Yules because their daughter rebuffed his advances. He did so anyway. The man is demented. Sarah was apologetic and hoped, since her involvement happened a long time ago, that I could forget about it and move on."

"What did you say?"

"I honestly didn't feel any sincere remorse from her. So I told her there was no way I could forget and move on, and that a person with her tendency for deceit was not anyone my partners and I would want working for our company. I fired her on the spot."

Leslie went back and sat down on the sofa. A part of her wanted to feel bad for Sarah, but all she could remember was how cruel Sarah had been at that night-club. "I'm sure she'll get another job."

"Not in LA. However, I suggested she follow her ex-boo to Paris. According to Cole, now that Longshire had to step down as CEO, that's where he's moving."

Sloan watched Leslie stand up and begin pacing again. Even in her red-and-green pj's with designs of Santa, reindeer, Christmas trees and candles, he thought she looked cute. He also thought, like he always did, that she had one hell of a figure.

Just looking at her in motion made him want her all over again, but he knew there had to be more to their relationship than lust. There *was* more. Now he had the important task of convincing her of it.

She suddenly stopped pacing and turned to stare at him. "I should have suspected something. If you recall, I mentioned to you that when Longshire came to my office, he knew you were once my boyfriend. We both wondered how he had known that when you and I hadn't been in contact in ten years."

"Come to think of it, considering what you told me about Longshire's relationship with your parents, it makes sense that he went after us all those years ago," Sloan said.

"How so?" she asked.

"He was engaged to your mother, but she eloped and married your father, right?"

"Yes."

"Then what better revenge than to have something similar happen to her daughter?"

When he saw that Leslie was no longer following him, he said, "It was my plan to ask you to marry me that week at the cabin during spring break."

"What! It was?"

"Yes," he said, seeing surprise on her face. She hadn't known. "That was my plan. I even bought the ring. I figured we would get married after you graduated."

"You wanted to marry me?"

"Of course I wanted to marry you, Leslie. I loved you and believed that you loved me. I figured marriage would be the next step for us."

"B-but you never mentioned marriage. We never

talked about it. I had no idea you wanted a future with me."

He leaned forward again, to make sure she understood. "That's apparently another mistake I made in not making sure you knew how I felt. However, in my defense, you told me plenty of times that you loved me, and I told you numerous times that I loved you. I figured that although you might not have known about my pending marriage proposal, you knew I wanted our relationship to continue beyond graduation. I had no intention of giving you up, Leslie. No intention whatsoever."

"But how did Sarah know you were going to ask me to marry you? Did you tell her what you planned?"

"No. I was so happy about it, though, I told Keosha, Tyler and Redford. I especially wanted Keosha to know so I could have an idea of your ring size."

He shifted his position on the sofa. "I spoke with Keosha yesterday and she admitted that in her excitement, she had mentioned it to Sarah. At the time she'd had no idea of Sarah's duplicity. When Sarah told Longshire, he probably thought it would be the ultimate revenge to hurt the daughter of his enemies the way they had hurt him."

Leslie nodded. "Evidently. And even after that worked, he still wasn't through with me and wanted even more revenge after Dad died." Suddenly, a huge smile spread across her face.

Sloan raised a brow. "What do you find amusing?"

"No wonder Martin Longshire was beside himself with anger that day he came to my office after finding out the identity of my new business partner. Taking my company away from me was supposed to be the ultimate revenge. The finale, so to speak. How do you think he felt knowing the man who ruined those plans was the same man he stopped me from marrying ten years ago? The same man Longshire assumed I would never be with again."

Sloan stood and crossed the room to stand in front of Leslie. "And that's where he made his mistake, Leslie. Because no matter how things ended between us, there was no way I could have stayed away when I found out you were in trouble. Undoubtedly, the man doesn't know the first thing about true love."

Leslie tilted her head back to stare up at him. "But you do?" she asked.

"I think so. I believe that even people in love make mistakes. And when they do, they should own up to those mistakes, admit they were wrong and apologize. I was wrong to leave you at the cabin without asking you to come with me to Walker's, and I apologize for doing it."

"Why did you?" she asked softly.

He broke eye contact with her for a minute. When he looked back at her, he knew he needed to try and explain how he felt. "Leaving me the way you did ten years ago hurt deeply, Leslie. It took me years to recover, and there were days when I wasn't sure I had. But I knew I had to help you out when I found out what Longshire planned to do. However, to protect my heart, I convinced myself I was doing it for my own kind of retribution. That's why I made that stipulation that you spend a week with me at the cabin."

He shoved his hands into the pockets of his slacks and said, "As you know, things didn't work out the way they were supposed to."

"We did sleep together, Sloan," she said. "That's what you wanted."

"Yes, but I was supposed to remain emotionally detached, and I couldn't do that. When we made love, I knew."

"You knew what?" she asked.

"That I still had deep feelings for you. That I still loved you. Discovering that made me feel vulnerable. I left the cabin to go visit Walker as a way to put distance between us and give me a chance to deal with what I was feeling. When I came back, you were gone."

In a soft voice, she said, "I couldn't stay at the cabin any longer, Sloan. Making love with you made me realize I still loved you as well. But I suspected it was one-sided and knew I had to protect my heart. I thought all we shared was a sex marathon."

"I told you there was more."

"Yes, but you never defined what 'more' was, Sloan, and I needed to know."

He squatted down and boxed her in with his arms on both sides of her. "Then let me define it now, Leslie. More means not just being a bed partner with you. It means you knowing that you are the woman I love, the only woman I could ever love. The woman I want in my life forever. More means sharing a life with you, having a family with you and you wearing my name. All the things I wanted to give you ten years ago, I still want to give you and with the promise that I will love you forever. It might be ten years in the making, but I believe we deserve our happy-ever-after."

Leslie fought back tears at Sloan's words. He loved her and ten years ago he'd intended to ask her to marry him. He *still* loved her.

"Leslie?"

She knew that now was the time to let him know just how she felt. "I do love you, Sloan. Even those years when we were apart and I believed you had betrayed me, I still loved you. That's why I could never become involved with another man. In all this time, you're the only man whose bed I've shared."

She saw the surprised look on his face. He straightened up to his full height. "Are you serious?"

"Yes, I am serious. The thought of another man making love to me was a total turnoff. That's probably why I was all in when we made love almost nonstop for two days. I was making up for lost time."

"And did you? Make up for lost time?" he asked as a smile touched his lips.

Leslie returned his smile. "Let's just say I tried." She stood and wrapped her arms around his neck. "I love you, Sloan. I love you so much."

She pressed her mouth against his. Tightening his arms around her, he deepened the kiss. The hard erection pressing against her middle said it all.

When Sloan finally broke off the kiss, she said, "Just think, Martin Longshire's plan failed, and we are back together. In the end, love won."

Sloan caressed the side of her face as he stared into her eyes. "Yes, sweetheart, love won. Our love won."

Leslie watched as Sloan took a step back, lowered himself to one knee and reached out for her hand. "I am about to do what I intended to do ten years ago. Will you marry me, Leslie?"

She threw her palm over her heart, shocked speechless. But it didn't take her long to recover. "Yes! Yes! I will marry you."

"And you won't make me wait, right?" he asked, sliding a ring on her finger.

She was in awe at how beautiful it was. "No, I won't make you wait."

"Good. And the reason it took me two days to get here is because in addition to flying to LA to confront Sarah, while I was there, I went shopping for your ring. I decided I could afford a more expensive one than the one I'd planned to give you ten years ago. I still have it and will give it to our daughter on her sixteenth birthday."

Leslie threw her head back and laughed. "Our daughter at sixteen? You are definitely thinking ahead, aren't you?"

"Yes," he said, wrapping his arms around her. "I would love to have a little girl who will grow up to be just as beautiful as her mother."

She shook her head, grinning. "If you say so."

"I do, and I can't wait to announce our engagement to the family. Most are headed for Denver this weekend to spend the holidays with our cousins, the Westmorelands. I'd like you to go with me. Will you go meet my relatives and spend Christmas and New Year's with me, Leslie?"

"I'd love to, Sloan. And you know what else I would love?"

"What, baby?"

"For you to make love to me."

Sloan then swept Leslie into his arms. "Which way to your bedroom, sweetheart?"

"Upstairs. The first door to your right."

And then, holding her tight, he took the stairs two at a time. Trembles rippled through her when he placed her on the bed.

He glanced around as he sat on the side of the bed to remove his boots. "Nice bedroom. You're still into yellow, I see."

"Um," she said, running the tip of her finger along his jeans-clad thigh. "Right now, Sloan Outlaw, I am into you, and more than anything, I want you into me. Literally."

"I am glad to accommodate you," he said, standing.

He quickly undressed and then returned to the bed to remove her pajamas. Heat flared all through her as he studied her naked body. She drew in a deep breath when he cupped her breasts.

"Sloan…"

She breathed out his name as he leaned in and began trailing kisses down her jaw and along her neck.

"Later for the foreplay. I need you inside me now, Sloan."

Leslie had dreamed of him every night since leaving the cabin, although she hadn't wanted to do so. And those dreams had been off the charts.

"I'll accommodate you now, but you know how I feel about foreplay."

Yes, she knew. He called it foreplay, but she thought of it as sensual torture. She watched him reach for his pants to retrieve a condom packet and then sheath himself, admiring his hair-covered chest and the trail that led down to his pelvis. She had accepted years ago that Sloan Outlaw was friggin' hot and overtly male. And from the look in his eyes, and the huge manhood between his legs, he was definitely aroused.

"You're going to owe me a whole lot of foreplay, Les."

Hearing him shorten her name made her loop her arms around his neck. "I have no problem with that, Sloan."

"Good."

No, *this* was good, she thought as she placed butterfly kisses around his mouth. He then lowered her to her back and eased into position on top of her while simultaneously opening her legs wider with his knee.

His manhood rubbed against her center, and the throb there made her eyes flutter closed.

"Look at me, Les. I want you to see me as well as feel me."

She fully opened her eyes to stare up at him, and what she saw in the dark depths of his gaze nearly took her breath away. She saw love, as deep as it could get, and she knew her own eyes displayed the same thing.

Then he entered her slowly, as if he needed to feel

every inch as he made his way inside. His tight, hair-roughened stomach pressed against hers as he continued to go deep, and deeper still, until their bodies were locked together so tightly there was nothing that could get between them.

She smiled, and he smiled back. Then he slowly thrust in and out as she moved her arms from around his neck to his shoulders, sinking her nails into his skin. If her action caused him pain, he didn't show it. Instead he picked up the rhythm, faster and harder.

That's when he leaned in and captured her mouth, kissing her in a way that had their tongues tangling nearly out of control. Each time she lifted her body, he plunged down, gripping her hips as he pounded into her.

She let out a scream at the exact moment he released a deep, guttural growl, and she knew this was only the beginning of forever.

Twenty

"Are you going to sleep in all morning, baby?" Sloan whispered close to Leslie's ear. He glanced out the window and saw it snowing. No surprise there. This was Alaska, after all.

He looked back down at Leslie and watched as she slowly opened her eyes. When she stretched her lips in a smile, he felt hunger stirring in the pit of his stomach.

"I'm exhausted," she said, closing her eyes again.

He didn't doubt it. After all, other than eating dinner, they had remained in bed and made love all through the night. He caressed the side of her face as love for her flowed through every bone in his body. "You want me to make you some oatmeal?"

She opened her eyes with a stern look on her face. "Stay out of my kitchen, Sloan Outlaw."

He chuckled. "Why? What harm could I do?"

"I'm not willing to find out." She glanced out the window. "It's daytime."

"Yes, and we only have four hours of it. I thought we could make some calls. I can't wait to tell everyone that I am marrying the most beautiful woman in the world."

"Oh, Sloan."

She wrapped her arms around him, and he pulled her closer in a long, drugging kiss. With her cradled beside him, Sloan took his cell phone and began making calls. With such a huge family, all he had to do was call specific individuals who would get the world out. Of course, it was Charm who asked the most questions. He couldn't help but smile. "Yes, Charm, Leslie and I are back together, and you're right. It is about time." He nodded. "I'll tell Leslie how happy you are to have another sister and that you welcome her to the family."

Glancing over at Leslie, he knew she was listening to his words, and he could see her fighting back tears. She might have lost her father, but she had gained a huge family who would adore her and love her as much as he did. When he finally ended the last call, the one to his cousin Dillon, he placed his phone aside and eased down in the bed.

"Tell me what you're thinking, baby." He saw the tear that fell from her eye, and he leaned in to lick it off her cheek.

"First you help save my company, then you want me as your wife and now you share your family with me. You make me feel so special, Sloan."

"That's because you are special. If nothing else, I

think being apart as long as we were has taught us not to take anything for granted. You mean so much to me, and I intend to spend the rest of my life showing you how much I love you."

He bent his head and kissed her, thinking he would never be able to show her often enough just what she meant to him. Since they were already naked, it didn't take him long to grab one of the condom packets he'd placed on the nightstand and prepare himself to make love to her.

They had decided they would start trying to make babies after the wedding. And since they intended to have a June wedding, when the weather wasn't as cold, that meant this time next year they would be making babies.

He'd already told her that she was what he'd wanted for Christmas this year, and he'd let her know what he wanted for Christmas next year. He wanted her pregnant.

He began kissing her, starting at her mouth and continuing down her body, making stops to tug on the hardened tips of her breasts and feast on her navel. She trembled beneath every area his tongue licked. Just tasting her skin had desire pumping through him. And when he made it to the area between her legs and buried his head between them, an intense hunger spread through him. His greedy tongue showed her just how much he wanted her, and it didn't take long for her body to respond with one hell of an orgasm.

"Sloan!"

He made his way back to her mouth, taking it with an urgency that he felt all the way to his toes. Then, releasing her mouth, he held her gaze as he slid inside her. "You still owe me a lot of foreplay, and I plan to collect, Les."

Her inner muscles clenched him as he began thrusting into her. "I love you, baby."

"And I love you," she said, running her hands over the muscles of his back.

Her touch made him thrust harder, and from the sounds she was making, he was doing it right. He broke eye contact with her to lean up and trail hot, moist licks along her neck and shoulders, her chin, and finally her lips. Pleasure erupted between them with a shared orgasm that rocked him to the core. She clung to him as much as he clung to her, and he knew at that moment he had definitely gotten what he wanted for Christmas.

A beautifully wrapped package named Leslie.

"Well, what do you think?" Sloan asked, pulling Leslie aside after he had introduced her to everyone. At least to those relatives she hadn't met yet.

"You were right. You and your cousin Derringer favor a lot, but I was able to tell you guys apart."

"There was no doubt in my mind that you would."

"I hope you don't expect me to remember names. This is a large family, and you are blessed to be a part of it. Everyone is so kind, and they are truly happy for us."

"Of course they are. Another Outlaw will be single no more."

Leslie glanced around the ballroom that was hosting the Westmoreland Charity Ball, not believing the number of people here. Most had arrived the day before

Christmas, like they had, and everyone stayed on Westmoreland property. There were plenty of rooms. She and Sloan were staying at the Westmoreland B&B. It had been a ranch that Jason Westmoreland's wife, Bella, had inherited and turned into a bed-and-breakfast. Leslie liked Bella, but then, she liked all the women in the family, those who were born Westmoreland or who'd married one.

Sloan's brother Garth and his wife, Regan, had announced they would be having a baby in the spring but assured them the baby would arrive before Sloan and Leslie's June wedding. Last night they'd gotten word that his cousin Delaney had given birth to twin boys.

However, the highlight of the night was when his cousin Bane and his wife, Crystal, announced they were expecting. And if the doctor's prediction held true, Bane and Crystal would be having their second set of triplets. They would be the first Westmoreland couple who'd managed such a feat, and they honestly seemed overjoyed about it. According to Sloan, the couple wanted a big family.

Everyone loved Leslie's engagement ring and thought she and Sloan made a beautiful couple. Leslie had to agree.

"Did I tell you today that I love you?" Sloan said, reclaiming her attention.

"Yes, but you can always tell me again," she said, smiling up at him.

"I love you, Leslie Cassidy, soon to be Leslie Outlaw."

She couldn't help but beam. "And I love you."

Not caring that they had an audience, Sloan pulled his future wife into his arms for a kiss.

Epilogue

A June wedding

With family and friends looking on, Sloan accepted the wedding ring from Garth, who was his best man. He then turned to his future bride to slide the ring on her finger while repeating the words the minister had instructed him to recite. "With this ring, I thee wed."

Once the ring was in place, he lifted her hand to his lips, sealing his vow with a kiss. He didn't care if what he was doing wasn't part of the program. He was a man who made his own rules. However, he did behave when she slid the wedding band on his finger. He noted she was wearing his wedding gift to her, the vintage aurora borealis bracelet with colorful crystals and diamonds. It looked good on her wrist and was a reminder of their time under the Northern Lights. Deep emotions hit him that he was finally marrying the woman he'd always loved.

He was ready for the part of the ceremony that pronounced them as husband and wife so he could kiss his bride. He would kiss her the way he wanted, and nobody better stop him. He thought she looked too beautiful for words in her bridal gown of white satin and lace.

His heart had nearly stopped when she entered the church on Mr. Yule's arm. The two had stayed in touch and formed a close friendship over the past six months. In addition to operating Cassidy Cosmetics, Sloan had brought her on to assist him in the running of his other businesses. For the time being, they had dual residences in both Wasilla and Fairbanks. She was grooming one of her junior executives to eventually take on more duties, since the cosmetics line was being expanded to the lower forty-eight.

"And by the powers vested in me by this great state of Alaska, I now pronounce you husband and wife."

Sloan didn't wait for the minister to give him permission to kiss his bride. He reached for Leslie and pulled her into his arms, giving her the only kind of kiss they would ever share. Long, thorough and possessive. Nobody interrupted, and he only released Leslie's mouth when he was good and ready.

He glanced over at the minister, who didn't seem the least bothered by Sloan's strong show of affection. In fact, Reverend Cross was actually grinning as he proceeded to announce, "I present to you, Sloan and Leslie Outlaw."

Among claps and cheers, Sloan swept Leslie off her feet and carried her out of the church. Once outside he placed her back on her feet and pulled her into his arms.

When he released her lips, she whispered, "You're so bad, Sloan Outlaw."

He grinned down at his wife. "Possibly, but I am also yours. Totally and completely, Mrs. Outlaw." He then pulled her into his arms for another kiss.

"Sloan definitely likes kissing you, girlfriend," Carmen leaned over to whisper to Leslie at the end of the wedding party's photo session.

Leslie couldn't help but smile. "And I love kissing him."

"Obviously. The two of you can't seem to keep your lips to yourselves," Carmen said, glancing around.

Leslie followed her friend's gaze and saw just where it had landed—right on Redford St. James, who was now being corralled by the photographer as Sloan took pictures with his best man and groomsmen. A sense of panic stirred Leslie's insides.

She had known Redford for as long as she'd known Sloan, since she'd met both guys the same day on the university's campus. Redford had been known around the university as a womanizer, and according to Sloan, Redford hadn't changed. If anything, he'd gotten worse.

"Carmen, I think I need to warn you about Redford," Leslie said, hoping it wasn't too late. She'd noted how taken her best friend had been with Redford last night at the wedding rehearsal.

"I know all about him, Leslie, so you don't need

to warn me. However, you might want to put a bug in Sloan's ear to warn Redford about me."

Leslie lifted a brow. "Why?"

A wide smile covered Carmen's face. "Because Redford St. James is the man I intend to marry. Your hubby is on his way over here, so I will see you at the reception."

Leslie watched Carmen walk off toward where Redford was standing. *Marry? Redford?* She hoped her friend was not biting off more than she could chew but had a feeling that she was.

"Are you okay, sweetheart?" Sloan asked, wrapping his arms around her.

She smiled up at him. "Yes, I'm fine." She decided to give him the warning from Carmen later. Right now, the only thing she wanted to do was concentrate on this man. Her Outlaw who would give her plenty of little Outlaws. It seemed she'd married into the right family. Not only was there a pregnancy announced practically every other month, but the Outlaws and Westmorelands had a knack when it came to multiple births. Garth and Regan had given birth to a little boy, and Cash and Brianna had twin sons. Sloan had jokingly told everyone he and Leslie would give Bart the first Outlaw granddaughter.

"You ready for your monthlong honeymoon to begin?" Sloan asked her.

She couldn't help but smile up at him. "Are you sure you want to do all that driving?"

He chuckled. "I am sure."

They would first take a road trip from Alaska to the

lower forty-eight through Canada, which was something they had always talked of doing while in college. When they reached New York, they would switch the rental car for a private jet. From there Sloan would fly them to Belize, where they would spend the remainder of the month.

"Are you ready to leave for our wedding reception?" she asked. "Things won't get started until we arrive."

"They can wait a minute," he said, and then he pulled her into his arms for yet another kiss.

* * * * *

*Get ready for Jess Outlaw's story,
coming in April!*

What Happens on Vacation…

Only from New York Times *bestselling author
Brenda Jackson
and Harlequin Desire!*

WE HOPE YOU ENJOYED
THIS BOOK FROM
HARLEQUIN
DESIRE

*Luxury, scandal, desire—welcome to
the lives of the American elite.*

Be transported to the worlds of oil barons, family dynasties,
moguls and celebrities. Get ready for juicy plot twists,
delicious sensuality and intriguing scandal.

6 NEW BOOKS AVAILABLE EVERY MONTH!

#2845 MARRIED BY CONTRACT
Texas Cattleman's Club: Fathers and Sons
by Yvonne Lindsay

Burned before, rancher Gabriel Carrington wants a marriage on paper. But when one hot night with fashionista Rosalind Banks ends in pregnancy, he proposes...a deal. Their marriage of convenience could give them both what they want—if they can get past their sizzling chemistry...

#2846 ONE LITTLE SECRET
Dynasties: The Carey Center • by Maureen Child

Branching out from his wealthy family, black sheep Justin Carey pursued a business deal with hotelier Sadie Harris, when things turned hot fast. Meeting a year later, he's shocked by the secret she's kept. Can things remain professional when the attraction's still there?

#2847 THE PERFECT FAKE DATE
Billionaires of Boston • by Naima Simone

Learning he's the secret heir to a business mogul, Kenan Rhodes has a lot to prove. He asks best friend and lingerie designer Eve Burke to work with him, and she agrees...if he'll help her sharpen her dating skills. Soon, fake dates lead to sexy nights...

#2848 RETURN OF THE RANCHER
by Janice Maynard

After their passionate whirlwind marriage ended five years ago, India Lamont is shocked when her mysterious ex, businessman Farris Quinn, invites her to his Wyoming ranch to help his ailing mother. The attraction's still there...and so are his long-held secrets...

#2849 THE BAD BOY EXPERIMENT
The Bourbon Brothers • by Reese Ryan

When real estate developer Cole Abbott's high school crush returns to town, she has him rethinking his no-commitment stance. So when newly divorced Renee Lockwood proposes a no-strings fling, he's in. As things turn serious, will this fiery love affair turn into forever?

#2850 TALL, DARK AND OFF LIMITS
Men of Maddox Hill • by Shannon McKenna

Responsible for Maddox Hill Architecture's security, Zack Austin takes his job very seriously. Unfortunately, his best friend and the CEO's sister, Ava Maddox, has a talent for finding trouble. When Ava needs his help, he must ignore every bit of their undeniable attraction...

SPECIAL EXCERPT FROM

ⒽHARLEQUIN
DESIRE

*Learning he's the secret heir to a business mogul,
Kenan Rhodes has a lot to prove. His best friend,
lingerie designer Eve Burke, agrees to work with him...
if he'll help her sharpen her dating skills.
Soon, fake dates lead to sexy nights...*

Read on for a sneak peek of
The Perfect Fake Date,
by USA TODAY *bestselling author Naima Simone.*

The corridor ended, and he stood in front of another set of towering doors. Kenan briefly hesitated, then grasped the handle, opened the doors and slipped through to the balcony beyond. The cool April night air washed over him. The calendar proclaimed spring had arrived, but winter hadn't yet released its grasp over Boston, especially at night. But he welcomed the chilled breeze over his face, let it seep beneath the confines of his tuxedo to the hot skin below. Hoped it could cool the embers of his temper...the still-burning coals of his hurt.

"For someone who is known as the playboy of Boston society, you sure will ditch a party in a hot second." Slim arms slid around him, and he closed his eyes in pain and pleasure as the petite, softly curved body pressed to his back. "All I had to do was follow the trail of longing glances from the women in the hall to figure out where you'd gone."

He snorted. "Do you lie to your mama with that mouth? There was hardly anyone out there."

"Fine," Eve huffed. "So I didn't go with the others and watched all of that go down with your parents and brother. I waited until you left the ballroom and went after you."

"Why?" he rasped.

He felt rather than witnessed her shrug. The same with the small kiss she pressed to the middle of his shoulder blades. He locked his muscles, forcing his head not to fall back. Ordering his throat to imprison the moan scrabbling up from his chest. Commanding his dick to stand down.

"Because you needed me," she said.

So simple. So goddamn true.

He did need her. Her friendship. Her body.

Her heart.

But since he could only have one of those, he'd take it. With a woman like her—generous, sweet, beautiful of body and spirit—even part of her was preferable to none of her. And if he dared to profess his true feelings, that was exactly what he would be left with. None of her. Their friendship would be ruined, and she was too important to him to risk losing her.

Carefully, he turned and wrapped her in his embrace, shielding her from the night air. Convincing himself if this was all he could have of her—even if it meant Gavin would have all of her—then he would be okay, he murmured, "You're really going to have to remove 'rescue best friend' off your résumé. For one, it's beginning to get too time-consuming. And two, the cape clashes with your gown."

She chuckled against his chest, tipping her head back to smile up at him. He curled his fingers against her spine, but that didn't prevent the ache to trace that sensual bottom curve.

"Where would be the fun in that? You're stuck with me, Kenan. And I'm stuck with you. Friends forever."

Friends.

The sweet sting of that knife buried between his ribs.

"Always, sweetheart."

Don't miss what happens next in
The Perfect Fake Date *by Naima Simone,*
the next book in the Billionaires of Boston series!

Available January 2022 wherever
Harlequin Desire books and ebooks are sold.

Harlequin.com

Get 4 FREE REWARDS!

We'll send you 2 FREE Books plus 2 FREE Mystery Gifts.

Harlequin Desire books transport you to the world of the American elite with juicy plot twists, delicious sensuality and intriguing scandal.

FREE Value Over $20
